EMMA'S MARSHAL

HARTS OF THE WEST

SAMANTHA THOMAS

ALSO BY SAMANTHA THOMAS

HARTS of the WEST Series

Emma's Marshal: Book One

Micah's Honor: Book Two

Gideon's Vow: Book Three

Ben's Gamble: Book Four

TALISMAN SERIES

HEALING HEARTS: Book One

DETERMINED HEARTS: Book Two

FORGIVING HEARTS: Book Three

www.SamanthaThomas.com

For my Emma

1

Emma wanted to look away, but she couldn't. She was drawn to the stranger like a moth to a flame. He must be new to town or passing through; that fact could not be in question. A man like that, she would have remembered.

He was leaning against a post on the boardwalk outside the lawyer's office, several days' growth darkening his cheeks, and crystal blue eyes peering from beneath the brim of his hat. There were two pistols hanging from his gun belt, both strapped down. Confidence emanated from every pore, and from the moment she turned onto Main Street, he'd been watching her progress.

Emma felt flushed, but it had little to do with the cloudless sky above, and everything to do with this stranger. She had never experienced anything like this before, and she wondered if she was turning into one of those swooning women she'd only heard about.

For the first time, Emma wished she had taken a little more care with her appearance before jumping in the wagon with her brother Luke and their niece Tilly. The dress she was wearing wasn't her best, but it had been perfect for weeding in the garden. Emma wasn't normally prone to such vanity; she preferred to leave that to their brother Rhett. However, in this moment, she conceded that a little more effort on self-care would have been wise. How could she have known there would be anyone other than the same old people on the streets of Autumn Springs?

"Emma! Watch where you're going! You plumb near took my thumb off."

Whipping her head forward, Emma readjusted her grip on the reins, neatly avoiding the next rut in the dusty road. Glancing over, she could see her brother Luke still glaring at her.

Emma arched one brow. "You're sure whittling is a good idea right now?"

"Not anymore," he huffed. "But I promised Tilly I'd make her a whistle. Right, Tilly?"

"Yes, sir!" piped a voice from the back of their wagon.

The last thing that child needed was a noisy whistle, but that wasn't a battle Emma was interested in fighting. Just keeping shoes on her eldest brother's daughter was enough. As long as Luke hadn't noticed the reason for her distraction, Emma wasn't going to say a word.

Resisting the urge to look back, lest the stranger see her crimson cheeks after her misstep with the horses, she continued to the mercantile. She decided to sweep the mysterious man from her mind. Her curiosity would do her no good; Autumn Springs didn't have men like that. Emma knew that better than anyone. She'd lived here her whole life, never having traveled farther away from her family land than town. Travelling in her dreams after reading one of her books didn't count. She would only take a peek and then move on. The stranger was probably passing through on his way to somewhere interesting. Anyplace had to be more exciting than Autumn Springs.

Emma wiped off the dust that had collected on her dress before she entered the mercantile. Mrs. Garvin wouldn't appreciate half the dirt from their ride in on her floor. Luke lifted Tilly from the wagon before the little girl could jump down on her own and then turned to Emma.

"I'm going to swing by the telegraph office. I want to see if there's any word from Micah."

Emma nodded. "Sounds good. You can meet us back here."

She knew that Luke was anxious for word from his twin, as was the rest of the Hart family. It felt so long ago that Micah had left the ranch as a young cowboy with a dream, and now he was coming back, dream fulfilled, as a full-fledged doctor. Having Micah home again would make the family feel complete once more.

With Tilly hanging on the handle, Emma pushed open the decorative glass door of the Garvin Mercantile. They were met with the beaming smile of Mrs. Garvin as she popped her head up from her work behind the counter.

"Girls! It's so good to see you." She bent down to take a closer look at Tilly. "And look how much you've grown! Such a beauty."

"My friend, Early—he's a real cowboy, you know—he says I'm growing like a weed, but not as useless."

Mrs. Garvin chuckled at the little girl's candor as she straightened wiping her hands on her apron. Emma gave her an apologetic look. "We may be lacking some refined feminine influence out at the Double H."

"With all those brothers of yours, I don't doubt it at all. Though all any of them would need to do, is announce he was looking, and there would be a line-up of ladies from across the territory." She waved her own words away. "I know, none are looking. Not to worry, if this little miss turns out anything like you, Emma, then she'll be just fine"

Turning back to Tilly, she gestured to the back door of the store. "Why don't you go take a look out back. You came at the right time. Our collie Maisie just had a litter of pups a few weeks back and ..."

Mrs. Garvin didn't bother finishing her sentence. The young girl was already long gone.

Emma laughed. "Don't think you're sending one of those pups home with us. We have more than enough critters about the place. The last thing Gideon wants is his daughter bringing home another thing that will end up underfoot."

"I wouldn't dream of it, my dear," claimed the store-keeper, with a wink. "Now, speaking of Gideon ..." Mrs. Garvin looked back to see that Tilly was still outside. "Do you think he'll ever remarry? It's been years now, and that child deserves a mother."

Some might have found the question rude or intrusive, but Emma knew it came from real concern for both Gideon and Tilly. Emma's mother and Mrs. Garvin had been close friends and she looked on all the Hart children as her own. Gideon had lost his wife in an accident two years prior and was refusing to move on.

Emma shook her head. "I honestly don't know, and he's quick to silence any discussion on it. I guess it will have to be the right woman who comes along to open his heart again."

"Well, he'll certainly have his pick when he's ready." Giving Emma's hand a brief squeeze, she continued. "I know I just said it, but your brothers are the most eligible bachelors in these parts. How they've all avoided that walk down the aisle is beyond me."

Emma gave a little laugh, knowing the full truth in those words. "They spend all their time making sure I suffer the same fate. I swear, I'll never find a man who is acceptable both to them and to me."

"Oh, those boys are just looking out for you, as they should. Making sure you find a man worthy of you, and who will make you as happy as the major makes me, and your father made your sweet mother. Bless their souls."

That was exactly what Emma dreamed of, but as the years passed, it seemed less and less likely.

"Autumn Springs has a plethora of men, Mrs. Garvin, but they're either too afraid of my brothers to even try courting, or they think I'll never be demure enough. Too tall and too blunt to make a suitable wife." Emma gave a half shrug. "And since I have no plans on settling, what I'm left with can only be described as inadequate options."

"Certainly, don't change on account of any man. My major loved me for exactly who I was, and we've never looked back. If a man lacks the courage to face the Harts or only wants a wilting wallflower, then he's not the man for you. It's as simple as that."

"That sounds good, but it doesn't always feel that simple, Mrs. Garvin."

"Emma, honey, mark my words. One day the right man will just walk in, and you won't know what hit you. Boom! Like that." The matter settled in the shopkeeper's mind, she turned to business. "Now, how about I grab that list you came here with, instead of talking your ear off. You look around and see if anything else catches your eye."

"I'm sure there will be something. There always is."

Emma busied herself perusing the store and marvelling at all the wonderful new things that Mrs. Garvin had ordered in since the last time Emma had been here. There was so much to look at. From books to tiny trinkets, Emma wondered about all the places the different items had come from. One day she wanted to see those places for herself.

There was a whole shelf of bottles and jars of products claiming to cure all sorts of ailments. She grabbed a jar of cream that professed its soothing help for tired eyes. Teresa La Baena—the foreman's wife and the Harts' cook—had mentioned that her eyes were bothering her as of late. Emma wondered if this might help.

As she lifted off the top to smell the cream inside, the bells on the mercantile door chimed. The sound startled her, and Emma ended up with cream on the tip of her nose. She looked up to see who had entered.

The stranger! What was he doing in here?

Even taller than she had presumed, the man seemed to fill the small store with his presence. He touched a finger to the brim of his dark hat and sent her a smile that carried a hint of amusement.

Realizing that the cream was still on her nose, Emma quickly wiped it away, and with glowing cheeks, she returned his smile. For the first time in her life, Emma Hart had absolutely nothing to say. Her brothers would never have believed it possible, but she had been struck silent. Her normal confidence had flown out the door as soon as the handsome stranger walked in.

"Good day, sir! If you give me a moment, I will be right with you. I am almost finished with Miss Hart's order."

Emma could not have been more grateful when Mrs. Garvin popped her head from around the back storeroom.

The stranger flashed another friendly smile, this time to Mrs. Garvin. "Not a problem, ma'am. Take your time." His astonishingly blue eyes glanced back at Emma. "I don't mind waiting here at all."

The storekeeper first raised an eyebrow at the man, then gave a slow smile and nodded before returning to the back room.

Was this man flirting with her? It had been so long that Emma wasn't sure, but it certainly felt that way. Once Mrs. Garvin had given away her last name, she expected it would have been the end of any interaction. Her family held a lot of sway in the Montana Territory, but this man had not been dissuaded. He acted like the name Hart didn't mean a thing. It was quite refreshing.

Not sure how to react or what else to say, Emma moved to turn away from the stranger when he addressed her again.

"Eyes bothering you?"

Emma gave him a quizzical look. "I beg your pardon?" The only eyes she could think of in that moment belonged to the man speaking, and staring into to them, the last thing she felt was bothered.

The man nodded towards the jar of cream that was still in her hands, that had only moments before been gracing her nose. "Oh. No."

"Good. I was going to say, you might be using it wrong." His mouth revealed perfectly white teeth as he grinned at her.

He was teasing her! If this had been one of her brothers, she would have thrown back a sarcastic retort, but in this moment, with this man, Emma found herself quite enjoying it.

"Your advice would have been sound, but this is for our cook, Teresa. I thought it would be a nice gift."

"Is it her birthday?" he asked.

"No, I just thought it might be useful."

"That's mighty kind of you, Miss ... Hart, is it?"

"Yes. Emma Hart." As she spoke, she waited for his reaction, the realization she was that lady, the one that came with five overprotective brothers.

But his smile only grew. What was it about those even teeth and twinkling eyes that made her catch her breath? Emma felt an unusual flutter in her chest. And when she found herself unconsciously twirling a lock of hair that had escaped from her bonnet, she quickly dropped her hand down to her side. With his coal-black hair and startling blue eyes, she was certain that he was the most handsome man she had ever laid eyes on.

"Well, Miss Emma Hart, it's a pleasure to make your acquaintance. My name is Weston Hayes. Though, you're most welcome to call me Wes."

Call me Wes. She may be feeling things that she had never felt before, but she hadn't yet lost her mind.

Emma smiled. "It's nice to meet you, *Mr.* Hayes." She placed all the emphasis on that last part. Despite the fact that he had her head spinning, he needed to be reminded that it was much too soon for such familiarity. He gave a low chuckle in response and nodded. Her point was received and noted.

Silence fell between them, but neither looked away. It was only when Mrs. Garvin reappeared, placing Emma's packages on the counter, that the spell holding them was broken.

"Ring them up, Emma, or on the account?"

"Our account. But feel free to help this gentleman. I'm waiting on Luke, and Tilly is still out back."

Mrs. Garvin laughed. "I took a quick gander out the window; she doesn't seem to be in any hurry to leave those pups."

Shaking her head, Emma replied, "I warned you. I'm

going to have to pat her down before we leave here. I'm likely to find a stowaway in one of her pockets."

The man laughed at her retort, which turned Mrs. Garvin's attention to him. "What can I do for you today, sir?"

Not wanting to eavesdrop, Emma turned her attention to the bolts of cloth that was carried in the fabric section of the store. She thought she was doing quite well at appearing to mind her own business, when there was a sudden commotion and Tilly appeared, marching through the store.

Holding a wriggling bundle of black and white fluff in her arms, Tilly stood before Emma, her blond hair a tussled mess. "Isn't she the prettiest, Auntie Emma?"

Emma peered down at the little pup in Tilly's firm grip. "He certainly is," she agreed.

Tilly held up the tail end of the pup for closer inspection. "Oh." Then she squeezed him back close to her chest. "Isn't he the handsomest boy you ever seen?"

"Ever saw," sighed Emma, as she blushed at Tilly's frank demonstration. There was no denying she was a country girl. "And while he is absolutely adorable, he will not be joining us on the ride home."

"Why not? Don't you love him? I love him." She stared up at Emma with those big blue eyes. Her niece wasn't giving up quite yet.

"It's not about me loving him, sweetheart. It's about his own mama loving him. He's too little to take away from her right now."

"Oh." Tilly looked crestfallen, but to her credit, she didn't complain or whine. "I understand. He should be with his mama."

Tilly's words tore at her heart, and Emma resolved to talk to her brother Gideon again.

During their discussion, Mr. Hayes completed his transaction and walked over to Tilly with two bags of sweets in his hand.

"If it's okay with your auntie, I'd be happy to share a candy with you."

Emma nearly laughed out loud at the pleading look on Tilly's face. She hated to disappoint her twice in as many minutes.

"You may, but you'll need to make sure that dog doesn't get to it first," replied Emma.

Tilly looked down at the pup and back over to the proffered candy. She seemed to be held hostage by the situation. It was Mr. Hayes who stepped in with a solution.

"How about I hold the puppy while you enjoy the candy?"

Tilly narrowed her eyes at Mr. Hayes. "Will you promise not to keep him? When he's bigger, he's going to be my dog." She then gave the pup's furry head a big kiss, which was returned with an energetic lick on her cheek.

It was clear to Emma that both dog and child had already made their minds up about each other. Mr. Hayes' assistance was probably only putting off the inevitable, but she was still grateful.

"I promise," said Mr. Hayes.

"Pinky swear?" asked Tilly.

Mr. Hayes held out his little finger. Once the pact was made, he lifted the puppy from Tilly's arms. He held out the candy bag with his other hand.

The little girl's eyes opened wide. "That's an awful lot of sweets, mister. Auntie Emma says that all that sugar will rot your teeth. Gotta look after your teeth, you know."

"Oh, she does, does she?"

Emma gently cleared her throat. "Yes, I may have said something to that effect."

"Your aunt is right. That's good advice. I have a terrible sweet tooth, so I have to clean my teeth all the time."

Tilly peered up at his face, checking the truth of his statement for herself. "They do look pretty good." Bored with the direction the conversation had taken, Tilly tugged on Emma's dress. "Do I have to say grace 'fore I eat this?"

"No, but you do need to thank Mr. Hayes," she prompted.

"Thank you, Mr. Hayes!"

"You're welcome, Miss Tilly."

Emma felt herself being drawn in by the scene playing out before her. She couldn't stop herself from hoping that Mr. Hayes would be sticking around Autumn Spring.

"You are most kind, Mr. Hayes. Thank you," said Emma. She didn't think she wanted the conversation to end just yet.

"Would you care for one yourself, Miss Hart?"

"No, thank you."

"I really do look after my teeth, you know." Apparently, Mr. Hayes felt it necessary to defend his purchase.

Emma didn't bother holding in her smile. "I'm glad to hear that, Mr. Hayes, but your habits are not for us to judge."

"Well, you do seem to be passing down sensible advice, and the truth is, I probably shouldn't eat these as often as I do. I find I use them to pass the time." The bell to the mercantile jingled as Mr. Hayes spoke again. "In my business, I don't often run into someone as lovely as you, Miss Hart. I appreciate the distraction...far sweeter than candy."

Mrs. Garvin, who had been silent until now, cleared her throat loudly. Emma and Mr. Hayes turned to see who had come through the door.

Her brother Luke stood glowering in the doorway. "If it's a distraction you're looking for, mister, how's about you step outside with me."

"Luke!" cried Emma. "Stop it!" She turned to Mr. Hayes. "I apologize for my brother, Mr. Hayes."

"I didn't mean to ruffle any feathers. My apologies," he replied.

Emma looked over to her brother, whose hand was now clenched. "Mr. Hayes, it was a pleasure to meet you. I hope you enjoy your time in our town."

"Not too much and not for too long," growled Luke.

Mr. Hayes tipped his hat to her brother in acknowledgement.

Emma lifted her order with a nod of thanks to Mrs. Garvin and took her leave, shooing her brother and a waving Tilly out the door before Luke could cause more of a scene.

Despite the awkwardness of their abrupt departure, and Luke's scowl the entire ride home, Emma found herself smiling. Meeting Mr. Hayes had been the most fun she could recall having in quite some time. The last image of his apologetic face, holding that furball of a pup in his arms, was almost irresistible.

No matter how difficult Luke or any of her other brothers tried to make it, Emma was going to go back to Autumn Springs to find out more about Mr. Weston Hayes. Excitement like this didn't come along often in her world, so nothing was going to keep her from it.

2

W es had no idea where his mind had gone.

He couldn't fault Emma's brother for putting him in his place. If he had a sister, and some stranger became a little too familiar, he doubted he would have responded any differently.

A cool head had kept him alive all these years, and with one look at the full-figured, fresh-faced Miss Emma Hart, he'd nearly ended up in a street brawl within his first few hours in town.

Wes couldn't explain what had come over him. He'd seen the young lady when she first entered town. He was surprised to see such a pretty thing working the reins as though she were born to it. When he saw she'd entered the mercantile, it had taken significant effort not to run down the boardwalk to join her.

What was it about Miss Emma Hart that had set the heat in his gut and the fresh talk on his tongue? There had been plenty of pretty faces in all the towns he had passed through, but this girl, this woman was different. This one had made him act the schoolboy. Wes might as well have pulled on her braids. If she'd had them.

Thinking of her hair, he wondered if those thick dark locks that had escaped from her bonnet were as soft as they looked. Were the unruly strands indicative of the woman they belonged to? Soft and lush, or more matching that mischievous sparkle she tried to hide in her eyes?

Emma was tall for a woman, nearly up to his chin, while most never made it past his shoulder. She was a beauty to be sure, and the simple cotton dress she wore did nothing to hide that fact. In fact, it only added to it. Her brother was right to keep an eye out for her. In any other town, the men would be drawn to a gal like that like flies to honey, yet here, in Autumn Springs he seemed to be the only one looking. That she was still a 'miss' rather than a 'missus' was just as surprising.

No, Miss Emma Hart was a bit of a mystery, and that made her all the more interesting. She didn't have the look of a town girl, with their frilly parasols and batting eyes, nor was she some soddie farmer's daughter. Those horses she'd been driving would have cost a pretty penny.

No, there was certainly more to Miss Hart than met the eye, but his interest had to end here.

Thinking that it would be the last time he saw the lady, Wes couldn't help but admire the figure she cut as she walked away.

The *swack* of a fly swatter hitting the counter behind him knocked him from his reverie.

"Is there anything else I can help you with, sir?"

The woman had a firm look of disapproval on her face as she brushed away the nonexistent fly. Despite the look, Wes was sure he could see a slight glimmer of humor in her eyes.

"No, ma'am." Wes held up his bag of sweets. "This is all I came for, thank you. But perhaps I can return this little fella."

He held out the squirming puppy to the storekeeper, who came around the counter to take it.

"My name is Mrs. Garvin, ..." She trailed off and waited patiently. Wes knew she wanted him to respond in kind.

"Ma'am. My name is Weston Hayes, Deputy US Marshal. Pleased to meet you and grateful your store was stocked to supply my sweet tooth."

Mrs. Garvin squinted across at him with one eye closed, like that might help her take the measure of him.

"Ma'am?"

"May I give you some advice, Marshal?" she asked.

Wes could see she was going to give it whether he agreed or not. "Yes, ma'am. I've always found there's much to be learned from the words of a smart woman."

Mrs. Garvin preened but he could see she wasn't easily fooled by sugary words. "I can see you have a way with you, but know that Miss Emma Hart is a good, kind, God-fearing girl. Don't let that confidence of hers have you thinking she's something she's not."

It hadn't even crossed his mind that Emma was anything more than a lady. Strangely, he was comforted to know that she had the townsfolk looking out for her. "I wouldn't dare, Mrs. Garvin."

"Good. But know this, lawman. Miss Emma can take care of herself, but that girl also comes with a posse of her own. Five brothers." Mrs. Garvin held up five fingers in case he needed a visual aid "There's not much those boys wouldn't do to protect their little sister."

Wes looked back to where Luke had been standing only a few minutes before. "They all built like that one?"

That made the woman laugh out loud. "You're a fair size yourself, but Luke is the youngest of the lot, Marshal, and despite being bigger than most men in town, he's not the biggest Hart."

He joined her laughter with his own. "Point taken, ma'am. I appreciate your concern."

Mollified, she continued. "Don't think my worry only pertains to you. I'm not entirely selfless in this matter. I love those boys, and this town, and I don't need them facing off with a deputy US marshal on Main Street because you went about your courting the wrong way."

"Courting, ma'am?"

"Do they call it something else where you come from?"

"No, I don't believe they do, but I'm only here to do a job and then I'll be on my way. As I said, it was real nice to meet your Miss Hart, but I'll have to leave the courting to the locals."

Wes hoped he was clear. He didn't need any misunderstandings that got him chased out of town. He wasn't the courting type. Marriage was not in the cards for him, and he had known that long before he was of age to make any vows. The past had shown him that, and Wes wasn't about to change his mind now.

"I'm getting on in years, Marshal Hayes, but I'm not blind yet," responded Mrs. Garvin.

Wes had no idea what the storekeeper was talking about. He'd only just met Emma; appreciation didn't equate to matrimony, so he really didn't understand what Mrs. Garvin was implying. Stuck on how to respond, Wes decided that escape would be the best way to end this conversation.

"Well, thank you again for the sweets."

Wes tipped his hat and made his exit, to the soft laughter of Mrs. Garvin.

Standing on the wide steps outside the mercantile, Wes looked up and down the main street of Autumn Springs. There was a steady movement of people up and down the boardwalk, and enough wagons and horses on the dusty road that pedestrians had to look twice before crossing, lest they find themselves quickly under hoof.

Using his hand and hat to shade against the sun, Wes saw no sign of the departed Harts or their wagon. He found himself disappointed being denied one last look at the lovely Miss Hart.

Most folks who lived in the territory had at least heard of the Hart brothers, even if they had never dealt with them before. For Wes, it was his business to know who the big operators and landowners were, as they were often privy to information that helped him greatly in tracking down criminals. What he hadn't heard was that the Harts had a sister amongst the mess of brothers. He could see now why they were keeping her under lock and key.

He removed his hat and wiped his brow before donning it again. If he thought that simple motion would be enough to wipe away the pretty picture of dark brown eyes with the thick fringe of lashes to match, he was sorrily mistaken. Miss Emma Hart would need more than a plain dress and bonnet to cover up the fact she was a true beauty.

Wes inwardly kicked himself for his thoughts. He hadn't even been in town a day, and he had spent more time tracking Emma's movements than his quarry's. If he didn't pull himself together soon, he might lose his chance at the McCarty boys altogether.

Still holding the two bags of candy in his hand, Wes shook his head. He still had plenty in his saddlebag from the last town he'd been through. He'd only been looking for an excuse to go into the mercantile.

"You a gunslinger, mister?"

The small voice came from behind him, and Wes turned to see two young, towheaded boys, likely brothers.

Wes slid his coat to the side, revealing his badge.

"A marshal! Ha! Told ya he wasn't an outlaw," scoffed the older boy.

Focusing on the embarrassed smaller boy, Wes nodded. "I'm no outlaw, but it's smart to be wary." He gave one of the bags of sweets to the boys. "Here, you can have these, but next time you see someone who looks like a bandit, don't take the time to ask him."

Wide-eyed, the boys took the candy and ran off down the boardwalk. Wes shook his head with a chuckle and headed in the opposite direction. He needed to stop by the jail and let the sheriff know he was in town, and his reason for being in Autumn Springs.

3

Closing the door behind her, Emma walked across the porch to the older woman, who was slowly rocking back and forth in a wooden chair.

She kissed her soft cheek and motioned to the inside of the house. "I put the jam I brought on the table, Mrs. Bryson. It's one of our best batches." Emma didn't expect a response and continued. "I'm going to go over and talk to Nora now."

The woman gave Emma a brief smile, then went back to her rhythmic rocking as she stared out to the green grass swaying in the fields beyond.

As she walked through the pasture to meet her closest friend, Emma felt a great appreciation for the beautiful piece of land that Nora owned. In some ways, Emma was a little envious of the freedom Nora had but knowing its devastating cost, and the hard work it took to maintain the property, she silently reprimanded herself.

The whirring and the buzzing of Nora's bee colonies could be heard long before she was in hailing distance of her friend. She waved to catch Nora's attention, and laughing, Nora came over to meet her.

"Are you ever going to get over your fear?" asked Nora, as she brushed away a trailing bee buzzing near her ear with her hand. "They are not as scary as you think."

Emma shook her head. "You should know better than to try and fool me. I will simply appreciate the beauty and the fruits of their labor from a distance."

"They won't hurt you," Nora insisted.

"Ha! Have you forgotten it was bees that broke my arm? Because I assure you I have not," replied Emma.

"Oh, stop." Nora was really laughing now. "They did no such thing, and you know it. Those weren't even bees: they were wasps, and it was your own fault. If you hadn't been so curious about the inner workings of that nest, you never would have fallen out of that tree. We never should have been up there in the first place. We were lucky we didn't get attacked after you hit it with that stick."

"*You* were lucky. *I* broke an arm and got stung on the inside of my elbow on that same arm. I was miserable for weeks." Emma returned the laughter. The episode was one of many scrapes she had gotten into as a child.

"I thought Papa would whip me for sure, but with your poor arm, he mostly just felt sorry for you. And he appreciated your interest. I got off with a stern warning to think before I followed your lead," recalled Nora.

"I'm so glad that lecture didn't stick," giggled Emma. "You know, I still have that nest somewhere."

"Really?"

"Absolutely. After what I went through to get it, I certainly wasn't about to give it up."

Sharing more memories as they headed back to the Bryson's house, Emma realized how lucky she was, to have such a wonderful friend close by. Nora stopped briefly to squeeze her mother's hand as it rested on the arm of the chair she rocked in.

"I'm going inside to get Emma a jar of our honey, Mama. You can join us or keep enjoying the fresh air."

Not expecting Mrs. Bryson to respond, the friends headed indoors.

The modest house was always as neat as a pin, and once again, she marveled at how Nora managed to keep it all in order. Emma wasn't sure how she would fare in the face of such adversity.

"You know, I've always loved coming here. I declare your father knew exactly what he was doing when he put that window in," remarked Emma as she nodded her chin at the big window that was above the kitchen basin.

"That was Mama's doing. She said if she was going to be stuck in this kitchen, she wanted to have something pretty to look at. Papa told her what she needed was a mirror, not a window, if she wanted the best view."

Both girls giggled at the sweet memory.

"I'm glad she held out for the window," said Emma.

"That she did. I think she just liked watching Papa and those silly bees. But enough about all that." Nora placed the teapot, two cups of tea, and two slices of fresh bread between them on the thick, oak kitchen table. "The tea's not fresh, I could make another pot, but you didn't come to drop off jam and reminisce. I've known you too long and can see that you are fairly bursting at the edges to share some news. So, time to spill it."

Emma wasn't surprised at her friend's assessment. "Am I that predictable?" she asked.

"Predictable? Heavens, that's the last word I would use to describe Emma Hart. Courageous, yet headstrong. Stubborn and too curious for your own good. Shall I continue?" Nora said and smiled.

"Ouch! What happened to 'if you don't have anything nice to say'?"

"You're right: in that case, I'll finish with the fact that you are also incredibly kind and the most wonderful friend a girl could have. Better?"

"Much. I was starting to think I would have to take that jam home with me."

Nora moved the jar of fresh jam closer to her own slice of bread. "Please accept my immediate apology."

Laughter spilled out between them and echoed in the kitchen. There were so few women in the area, and once again Emma was reminded of her good fortune to have Nora in her life.

"Well, you're right; you almost always are. I've been dying to talk to you." Emma lowered her voice. "But you must promise not to tell a soul."

"And who would I tell?" replied Nora as she lifted her arms. "This is as exciting as my life gets."

"All right." Emma paused for only a second before she simply couldn't hold it in any longer. "There was a new man in town this morning."

Nora shrugged. "That's hardly news. Men are coming and going each day in Autumn Springs, like every other booming town. A new man is not a rare occurrence, Emma. Honestly, it feels like we are outnumbered ten to one here. You're outnumbered five to one in your own home. And don't get me started if we include the mining camps—"

"That is not the point! You—" Emma stopped when she saw the merriment in her best friend's eyes. "You're teasing me."

"I am," replied Nora. "Now, tell me everything but

remember to keep your voice low. Mama may be lost in her thoughts today, but she hears every word."

Emma didn't need any further encouragement.

"He had eyes like the bluest of skies, and dark black hair that curled just under his ears."

"Was he tall like your brothers?"

"As tall as Luke and Micah." Emma noticed Nora's faint blush at the mention of Micah's name. Emma was about to ask if she had heard from Micah when Nora interrupted with another question.

"Did you get his name?"

"Weston Hayes." Emma said it slowly. This was the first time she had spoken it aloud, and she liked the way it sounded rolling off her tongue. "He told me to call him Wes."

"You didn't!" Nora nearly choked on the tea she had started to sip.

"Of course not. But I did find out that he is good with puppies and children and has a terrible sweet tooth."

"That's more than a brief encounter. How on earth did he get past your brothers?"

"There was only Luke, and he was busy at the telegraph office, so it was just Tilly and me. We spoke for only a few minutes. Well, he mostly spoke, and I acted like a twitter-pated fool."

"Somehow I doubt that," said Nora mildly.

"It's true," moaned Emma. "All my confidence fled, and then Luke marched through the door, threatened him, I had to flee with Tilly so as not to cause a scene."

"Oh dear."

Emma smiled. "It wasn't that awful. While embarrass-ing, it was still the most exhilarating morning I've had in quite some time. It was far from the usual boring trips to town."

Nora shook her head at Emma's energy and lust for life. "And dare I ask where this man is now?"

Emma let out a long, dramatic sigh, then wrapped her hands around the dainty, flowered teacup. "Probably long gone. But I'm fully intending to find out, just to be sure. He didn't have the dress or look of a miner, and what wrangler do you know who has a day off to go to town to buy sweets? He wasn't a dandy either; he was wearing two guns and they didn't look like they were for show. He was just...all man. A real mystery."

"Oh no," sighed Nora. A real one.

"What do you mean 'oh no'?" asked Emma.

"What I mean is you, Emma Hart, just used the word 'mystery' and coming from you, that always means trouble's coming."

"That's not true." Emma wasn't sure she should be offended by Nora's assessment.

"Oh, yes, it is, Emma, and you know it."

"I know no such thing. And confess: wouldn't you be even a little bit curious?"

"I can honestly say there isn't a single man in all of Autumn Springs that I am the least bit curious about," declared Nora.

There was something in the way Nora stated her position so firmly that caught Emma's attention. Enough to make her push thoughts of Mr. Weston Hayes aside, if only for the moment.

"No one living 'in' Autumn Springs? Hmmm, how about one who grew up outside of town and will soon be living there again?"

Emma knew her guess had been correct when Nora's

cheeks once again flushed. She wondered why Nora was bothering to try and hide it from her. Something was going on.

"Aren't we talking about you right now?" It was obvious Nora was trying to divert her attention.

"We were. And if you would like to continue, I can tell you how when *I* was in town this morning, Luke stopped by the post office and sure enough there was a letter from *my* brother Micah. See, still talking about me."

"You're so helpful," said Nora as she gave Emma a sour face.

"Micah said that he should be home sooner than expected, and he has some exciting news. I'm hoping it's that he will be taking over Doc Owens' practice. It would be a blessing for all of Autumn Springs. Doc Owens must be ready to retire by now and, let's be honest, I'm not sure he ever really was a doctor, despite his claims. Hanging out one's shingle does not a real doctor make. At least a good one. Your father was the one we all turned to."

"True, Papa was hoping to put the medicine behind him and farm, but he could never turn folks down. I still have a poor soul or two out this way looking for help. I do the best I can, but it would be nice to have Micah practice back here."

Nora always had such a sunny outlook on life, it was easy to forget all that she and her family had gone through.

"Well, Luke especially is over the moon that his twin is finally coming home," Emma shared. "For all his tough talk, I know how deeply he's missed his other half."

Nora nodded. "Of course he is. I'm sure you are all happy to get such news."

Emma wasn't about to disagree. Micah's return had been a long time coming. "We are. It will be good to have *all* of us back together again."

Her friend didn't respond to the emphasis Emma had placed on the word all. She simply smiled. Emma didn't want to press her anymore. She would talk when she was ready. Nora knew that her ear was always available and her shoulder ready for when that time came.

Changing the subject, Emma and Nora continued to chat until their tea had disappeared. Emma took her leave with an extra jar of honey in her deep pocket.

The ride back to the Double H was uneventful and Emma was grateful for the quiet. Early, one of their long-time ranch hands, had taken Tilly out on her pony for practice, allowing Emma to sneak in the lone visit to Nora.

It also gave her plenty of time to think about the mysterious Mr. Hayes. In her thoughts, she was calling him Wes. He'd given her leave to do so, but she didn't need to let him know that she had accepted, at least in her head. "Wes" suited him, as she liked the way it sounded. It was silly to place any importance on a name, but Emma wasn't sharing that with anyone. It was her secret alone.

All she needed was an excuse to head back into town, and that wouldn't be all that difficult. She would need to do it soon. Otherwise, she was risking that Wes would be long gone from town. She didn't plan on anything untoward; she only wanted to satisfy her curiosity.

Perhaps after another conversation she would find him like many others, dull, and intimidated by her family, and she could dismiss him from her mind. Emma closed her eyes for just a moment and pictured his teasing blue eyes as he held on to the wriggly puppy in the mercantile. If her reaction to the man so far was any indication, her heart might already be lost.

~

"I GOTTA SAY, Sheriff, that Autumn Springs is a bigger town than I expected," remarked Wes, as he looked out the window and into the street. "It's got that feel of excitement in the air."

"Bigger town, bigger problems, and this place is growing by the day," replied Sheriff Wyley.

Wes looked past the white hat and matching mustache of the balding sheriff, to the empty cells behind him. "Business here doesn't look to be booming."

The older man gave a chuckle as he leaned back in his chair. "I'd take that as a compliment, but I also know that come payday, the mining boys and wranglers will be sure to keep this old man on his toes. Youth and full pockets are more than enough to keep me busy, Marshal." Cocking his head to the side, he gave him a long look. "Now, I'm guessing that you aren't here for the open deputy position. Why don't you tell me what's on your plate, and just how many of these five cells you plan on filling up."

Wes smiled. It was hard not to take a liking to the aging sheriff. He might be short on hair beneath that lawman's hat, but he hadn't lost his edge.

He pulled out the contract on the McCarty brothers from the pocket inside his woolen coat. "Just the two this time, Sheriff. You'll have plenty of room for when your young fellas hit the town."

He pushed the paper across the desk so Sheriff Wyley could take a look.

"Humph. McCarty, hey? Weaselly lookin' boys, that's for sure. That Felix has a face only his mama could love. He missin' an ear?" He held the paper away from his face, his eyes preferring the distance.

"He is," affirmed Hayes. "Took a close bullet a few years

back. Didn't lose his life, but lost his marbles, and his title as Belle of the Ball."

The sheriff snorted at Wes's attempt to be funny. "Hmph, can't say I've heard of them, and haven't seen them neither. You think they are in these parts?"

"Seems to be the direction they were headed. Rumor has it, they have kin out this way. Figure I'll start in town, then head out to the mining camp to ask around."

"You think they got work up there?" asked the sheriff.

"That's one thing I'm sure they haven't done. The McCartys haven't done an honest day's work in their lives," he replied.

"Well, I don't envy you the work. It's hard to find a man who doesn't want to be found." Sheriff Wyley looked down at the picture once again. "'Course, these two don't look all that bright."

"Isn't that why they pay us the big bucks, Sheriff?" Wes couldn't stop his mouth from twitching as he said the words.

That got the old man laughing, which then led to a coughing fit. Smoothing out his bushy white mustache, the sheriff pointed at Wes. "Good to see you still got your sense of humor, son. That's usually the first to go in this line of work. How much you gettin' for these boys?"

"One hundred for Felix, Two for Creed. I wonder if Felix will be insulted that he's not worth as much as his brother." He didn't care so much about the money. Anything he made was tucked away in the bank. He didn't have need for much, and no one to spend it on.

"Planning on bringing them in breathing, or should I inform our undertaker that he's about to get some business?"

Wes shook his head. "That's up to the McCartys, but my preference is always breathing. I'm not the one to mete out the justice, Sheriff, just the one to see it has a chance of being delivered."

The lawman lifted his brow at Wes' response. "Words of a moral man, I see. Unusual for a lot of men who wear that badge. We'll see how you feel in a few years. If you're still kicking, that is. I'd be curious if you still feel the same."

He nodded in response.

Wes wasn't insulted. The sheriff had been around long enough, and so had he, to know the truth of his words. Not all marshals were the same. Many spent as many years on one side of the law as they did the other. There were also times where weeks spent on a dusty trail, hunting godless men, led to moments where the law didn't always seem so clear. When the men he worked with allowed the judges Colt, Winchester or Sharp to pass sentence on unarmed men, he was done. Wes had walked away from his position with the Pinkertons.

His father had been a Pinkerton and, despite the devastation that job had wreaked on his family, Wes had followed in his footsteps. As the years went by, the line between right and wrong started to get blurred, and he could no longer tell which side of that line his superiors were standing on. Alongside the questionable apprehensions he'd seen, Wes wasn't comfortable with the money he saw exchanging hands, and so he'd taken the job with the marshal's office. As a deputy marshal, he could work on his own and could sleep with a clean conscience. Since that point, he had never looked back.

He changed the subject to address his most pressing need. "Any recommendations for a place to stay? I've had enough of my bedroll and was hoping for a real pillow for a night or two." He was also looking forward to fresh sheets and a real bed.

Sheriff Wyley fiddled with the end of his snowy mustache as he considered the question. "Depends on what you're looking for, Marshal. Saloon seems a popular choice for a young fella such as yourself—"

"I'll stop you there, Sheriff. That's not for me. All I'm wanting is clean sheets and some quiet."

The lawman smiled, and Wes was almost certain he could see approval in his eyes. "Well, if you're feeling flush, there's the International Hotel."

"International?" asked Hayes. Seemed a pretentious name for a town as small as Autumn Springs.

The sheriff gave another chuckle. "I believe Sam Matthews has big plans for his hotel, and all of Autumn Springs for that matter. Figures if the railway comes through these parts, he'll be set. Big dreamer, that one. 'Course it's men like them that grow these towns."

"Those my only two options?"

"No. There's plenty of rooming houses, but you get what you pay for. The place you're looking for is probably Mrs. Durnford's. Lost her husband in the mines, years back now, and set up a boarding house here in town. She's a God-fearing woman and don't put up with even a hint of nonsense under her roof. She runs a straight-up place and is likely your best bet. It's clean and fair-priced. She's also a fine cook."

Sheriff Wyley seemed certain about Mrs. Durnford's stellar qualities, so Wes wasn't going to bother look for anything else.

"Thanks, that sounds like exactly what I need."

"You can tell her that I sent you," added the sheriff.

Something in the way Wyley was talking about the woman had Wes wondering if the old lawman might be sweet on the widow. "Any other messages you might like me to send along, Sheriff?" Wes gave the sheriff a wink.

"Oh, don't give me that. Mention me or don't. It doesn't matter to me one way or another."

Like a boy caught with his hand in the cookie jar, the sheriff gave him a vexed look. Wes knew he had been right. The sheriff cared, he cared very much. Good for him.

"I'll let her know," said Wes, keeping a straight face, for the sake of the lawman's pride.

This time the sheriff only shrugged.

"Thanks again, Sheriff. I'll be heading to the mining camp tomorrow and then I will swing by your way again. Even if nothing pans out," said Wes.

The sheriff smiled at Wes's prospecting pun. "I'll ask around town, see if anyone has caught wind of your boys."

"I'd be much obliged. I'll be sure to let the widow Durnford know how helpful you've been," teased Wes as he tucked the picture of the McCarty brothers back into his pocket.

"Go on, get out of here now, Marshal. I've got work to do."

Touching the brim of his hat, he left the jail.

4

Wiping her brow to dispel the beads of sweat that had formed there, Emma once again wished she'd remembered to bring something to cover her head. With the sun blazing down on both her and Tilly while they fed the hogs, Emma was sure she could feel freckles forming. She could still picture her mother's exasperation as she ran outside as a little girl, hair flowing behind, Mother yelling after her that squinting in the sun would ruin her eyes. At least Tilly had the good sense to have grabbed her bonnet, although that was more likely due to Teresa catching her before she left the ranch house. Emma could have run back to the house or even have Tilly do so, but Emma wanted the chores done, and she didn't feel like wasting time over the fear of a few freckles.

"Someone's coming!" yelled Tilly, making sure she was heard over the grunting of the hungry hogs.

Emma turned, shading her eyes with her hand.

A solitary rider was headed towards the ranch house, but Emma didn't recognize them from such a distance. As the rider drew closer, she could see it was a man, and he must have spied her observing him, as he turned his horse in her direction.

As he got closer, Emma's breath caught in her throat. Tilly looked up to see why she had gasped.

It was him: Weston Hayes!

In the two days since Emma had met him at the mercantile, she had been unable to find a reasonable excuse to go back into town. She had tried telling herself to stop thinking about him, that he had likely already moved on. But here he was, riding towards her, and Emma knew that any efforts she made to push Wes from her mind were futile. Her pulse was already racing, and the man wasn't even standing before her.

"It's the man with the sweets, Auntie Emma. Remember?" asked Tilly.

Remember? How could she possibly forget? His startling blue eyes were the last thing she saw before she drifted off to sleep, both nights since they'd met.

"Miss Hart!"

Wes smoothly dismounted from his horse like a man born to the saddle and sauntered towards them. How a man could make the simple act of walking attractive was beyond her comprehension. Yet, here he was, proving it possible.

Emma patted down her skirt, wiped at the bits of feed that had attached themselves to her blouse, then attempted to tuck loose hairs back into her bun. She should have worn her apron, but that was in the same spot as her bonnet. Sighing inwardly, she wondered if there was ever going to be a time when Wes saw her looking her best. She didn't even want to imagine the picture she presented. Her mother and Teresa had both warned her there would come a time when she might want to put some care into her appearance. She had laughed it off each time, but was now beginning to see the wisdom in their advice.

"Miss Tilly." Wes lifted his hat briefly in the young girl's direction.

Emma was about to greet him, but Tilly spoke first. "You left my dog at the mercantile, right, Mr. Hayes?"

"Tilly," admonished Emma. "That is no way to greet our visitor."

Immediately repentant, Tilly muttered an apology and dug the toe of her shoe into the dirt.

Wes didn't leave the girl feeling guilty for long.

"A pinky swear is no small thing, Miss Tilly. Your pup is safe and still growing with its mama 'til it's ready for you."

"If!" interjected Emma, knowing full well she was fighting a losing battle. Still, she had to at least put in some effort on behalf of her brother Gideon. "Your father hasn't agreed to anything yet, young lady."

"He will," Tilly replied complacently.

Her niece was probably correct. Since losing his wife, Tilly's mother, there wasn't much he was prone to deny her. It was a miracle the child wasn't spoiled rotten.

"Welcome to the Double H Ranch, Mr. Hayes." Emma turned a bright smile in his direction. "I hadn't expected to see you again. To what do we owe the honor?"

"The honor is all mine, in the opportunity to see both of you lovely ladies again." He sent a wink down to Tilly, who gave a little giggle at the compliment. Emma had to remind herself not to do the same, lest her actions match those of the five-year-old old at her side.

"Is that your only reason for riding this far out of town, Mr. Hayes?" Emma knew that if he answered this very forward question with a yes, she would probably expire on the spot.

"I'm afraid not, Miss Hart. I'm here because I need to speak to your brothers."

"All of them?" Emma couldn't imagine what business would require all five. Well, she could, but that was too far-fetched for even her imagination. Emma knew that she was fair enough to look at, but no sane man would come courting after meeting a woman for only a few brief moments.

"No," he chuckled. The low rumble of his laugh sent a shiver right through her, which made no sense on such a hot day.

"Which one?"

"I guess whichever brother is in charge around here," replied Wes.

"I'm as much a Hart as my brothers, Mr. Hayes," Emma said peevishly, if you need some assistance with something, you can just as easily speak with me." Emma hoped she didn't sound too rude, but she also got tired of people looking past her as an equal sibling on the Double H.

"As much as I might like that, Miss...may I call you Miss Emma?"

Emma nodded. "You may."

"Well, then, Miss Emma, as much as I might like this conversation to continue, it's the one in charge of hiring I'm looking to speak with. And unless that's you..."

The way he spoke her name made it sound much prettier than Emma ever thought it could. It was hard to not watch his mouth as he spoke and wish for him to say it again.

"It's not. Normally that's under the purview of Mendo La Baena. He's our foreman. He's out in the east pasture with my brothers Rhett and Ben. I'm not sure when to expect them back. It depends on what they run into out there. My eldest brother, Gideon, is here, as is Luke." Emma tried not to blush in remembrance of Luke's threat in the mercantile. "I can take you in to see them."

"I'd be much obliged." Wes glanced over at the hogs. "If you can spare the time."

"It's not a problem, Mr. Hayes. They've all been fed."

Emma looked at Tilly and then to the pen of hogs.

"Now, Tilly, I'll let you stay out here if you promise me, you'll stay out of that pen?" Her niece gave her an unconvincing nod. "I mean it. You're not big enough to be in there, and those pigs would be happy to pass on their slops and enjoy a juicy little morsel like you."

Ignoring the choking sound from Wes as she threatened her niece, Emma continued. "Tilly?"

"Cross my heart," said Tilly as her finger swiped the wrong side of her chest. The little girl glanced over to the pen, then scrunched up her face. "Maybe I'll just go see Early instead."

As Tilly ran off, Emma called after her, "Don't get in the way!"

Tilly kept running.

When she turned back to face Wes again, she was met with a raised eyebrow. "When I met you at the mercantile, you were buying a fancy eye cream for your cook. I thought you were a kind woman. Two days later I witness you threatening a small child with swine violence. I'm starting to wonder which Miss Emma Hart is the real one."

Emma laughed. "Both, Mr. Hayes. I'm sure my brothers will attest to that fact."

"Duly noted," Wes said, nodding. "I'm surprised to see hogs on a ranch like this. I thought that cattlemen frowned upon the sheep and swine folk."

Emma tilted her head and looked up at Wes. "I don't see

why you could look down on anyone doing honest work."
She gestured to the pen. "We have a lot of hungry mouths to
feed here at the Double H. Hogs aren't picky about what
they eat, and they're mostly meat."

Wes chuckled at her response. "After that description, I
can only hope they don't have good hearing."

Smiling, Emma motioned to the ranch house. "Come
along. You can tie your horse at one of the hitching posts,
and I'll introduce you to Gideon. I'm not sure how much of a
welcome you might get from Luke."

She waited until he had circled his horse around and
started walking in step with him.

"I'll admit that I'd prefer to stay on the good side of the
fabled Brothers Hart, but if I'm being completely honest, I'd
have to say that it was worth risking Luke's ire to have the
chance to meet you," confessed Wes.

Emma's heart soared at his words. But she cast her eyes
downward so he wouldn't see how much it pleased her. He
wasn't too afraid of her family name or her brothers. Could
it be possible that he was feeling the same interest and
curiosity toward her as she was for him?

Emma was inexperienced at flirting and unsure of what
to say next. She decided to stick with a topic she was
familiar with.

"Impressive mount, Mr. Hayes. His muscles look more
iron than flesh."

"He doesn't turn twister at rattlesnakes, I'll give him
that," said Wes.

Emma shivered at the mention of her most hated foe. "I
wouldn't be so brave. I loathe snakes."

Wes grinned and rubbed the horse's cheek as they
walked. "I wouldn't claim he likes them either. Bass is his
name; he's a beauty. Bought him off a horse trader, years

ago. I swear he's only part broke, but he's never offered me any funny business and to this point he's tolerated me. We complement each other in many ways."

"You're a partially tamed man, Mr. Hayes?"

He stopped in his tracks, and it was only then by the look of amused surprise on Wes's face that she realized how her words might be interpreted.

"I didn't mean—"

"I am." His response was a husky rumble that rippled across her skin.

Emma was bold, but she was completely out of her element and knew it. She kept walking, ignoring all that just happened.

"Bass? That's an odd name for a horse," said Emma. She hoped he would be kind enough to pretend that her embarrassment hadn't taken place.

He was.

"He's named after someone I greatly admire, but I didn't want to call him Reeves. I thought that sounded too much like an English butler." Wes said, shrugging. "He's a great horse and a better companion than most people."

"I can't argue with that," laughed Emma. "So, tell me: are you staying in Autumn Springs for a while? Are you looking for a position here at the Double H? There are plenty of ranches in the area. What made you decide to ride out here? Are you—"

"Whoa there, Miss Emma. That's an awful lot of questions, and not much of a chance for answering."

"Sorry. Do you need me to ask them one at a time?"

Chuckling at her teasing response, he replied, "No, I think I managed to get them all." Wes kicked at a small rock in their path. "You're a mighty curious one, aren't you?"

"If you mean, am I interested in the goings on in the

world around me, then I guess the answer to your question would be yes. Yes, Mr. Hayes, I am a curious one." Emma waited for the expected response.

"Unusual for a woman," said Wes.

And there it was.

She sighed. The same reaction that most men had towards a woman who wanted to discuss anything other than cooking and needlework. While they found the topics dull, she was expected to limit herself to such, and to be interested in something more was considered odd.

Her previously soaring heart now began to falter, like a kite running out of wind.

"Why exactly is it unusual for a woman to be curious, Mr. Hayes?"

Wes almost startled at her sour reaction. He could tell he had taken a misstep but couldn't quite figure out where it had happened.

Emma let him squirm.

"Well—I, uh—Well, I just meant that most ladies, such as yourself, don't involve themselves in the, uh...business of others."

"Ah." replied Emma, as though his explanation had made it finally clear for her. "You mean that a lady takes care of the home and children, and the rest isn't her concern."

"Exactly!" Wes's strong, chiseled jaw, that had been clenched in worry, relaxed in a relieved smile. He seemed pleased that Emma had so nicely summed up what he had been trying to say.

She let out a very unladylike snort of disgust, and the smile on Wes's face vanished.

"What have I said now?"

"Nothing *unusual* for a man, Mr. Hayes," said Emma.

"What does that mean?"

"It means...oh, never mind. It doesn't matter what it means." Emma was about to explain the obvious to a man, who would never understand. Not that he was awful or unpleasant about it; he was a man, and that was all there was to it. She would have to show him that he was misguided, because telling him would only be interpreted as more women's prattle.

"It appears to matter very much to you, Miss Hart; therefore, it matters to me."

Wes had gone back to addressing her formally; Emma wondered if he was trying to convey his respect. He hadn't dismissed her concerns. Maybe she should give him the benefit of the doubt.

Emma waited as Wes tied off his horse then removed his gloves, tucking them into one of his saddlebags.

"Women are more than ornamental, Mr. Hayes. It's only men who think us purely decorative." She let the words hang in the air between them.

"I find you to be most beautiful, Miss Emma. I would be lying if I said otherwise. I would also have to be blind not to notice...despite the remnants of what looked to be delicious leftovers." Wes glanced down at the food stuck to her blouse. "But I don't recall describing you as ornamental at any point in our interactions."

She scratched at the bits that had dried to the cotton, then stopped. They were firmly adhered to the fabric across her ample bosom, and Emma didn't need to be drawing any further attention to such things.

His compliment and teasing helped to reduce her annoyance but she wasn't ready to give in quite yet. "Perhaps not in those words, but you did imply it."

Wes stepped in front of her, his eyes gazing deep into

hers. His face was so close, Emma could smell a hint of cinnamon candy on his breath. She felt her pulse quicken again at his nearness, and a warmth spread through her body, cumulating in her heated red cheeks. It was no longer irritation that had her heart pounding.

He took a loose strand of hair that had escaped her bun and tucked it behind her ear. "If I offended you, Emma, please accept my apologies. That was not my intention. You may ask me any questions you like."

His intimate use of her name and the closeness of their bodies had Emma audibly swallowing before she could speak.

"Thank you, Mr. Hayes." She had hoped it would sound confident, but her acceptance of his apology came out as a whisper. He was so close. Before she could stop it, her hand raised to her ear, touching the heat that still lingered there from his fingers. She expected him to step back, to remove himself from such close quarters, but he didn't move an inch. Emma wasn't sure she wanted him to.

The contrite look in his eyes disappeared and was replaced by something else that she couldn't name, but somehow, she still recognized it. Whatever it was, she was feeling it too. What was happening?

With a throaty groan, Wes suddenly pulled himself away. In that moment, Emma felt bereft like she had lost something that she desperately wanted to keep. None of what she was feeling made sense. She blinked and gave her head the slightest of shakes, hoping to settle the emotions that were swirling like a twister in her head.

She cleared her own throat, then spoke. "Perhaps we should go inside and see Gideon and Luke."

"Yes." Wes's voice was low.

"I...I will need to go back and check on Tilly." Emma

didn't know why she was still talking, but she didn't know what else to do. "This way, please, Mr. Hayes." She pointed to the large wood and stone ranch house with a huge wrap around veranda.

Emma led the way into the big house and towards the office, where she knew Gideon and Luke had ensconced themselves earlier. She knocked but didn't wait for an answer before entering.

Both men looked up at the disturbance. Gideon with question and Luke with irritation when he saw who it was. It was Luke that first addressed Mr. Hayes.

"You! What are you doing here?"

Emma gave her youngest brother a glare that quelled any further outburst. She introduced Wes before Luke could decide he needed to say anything further.

"Gideon, this is Mr. Weston Hayes. He's new to Autumn Springs and has just arrived at our door, wishing to speak with you."

"Thank you, Miss Emma. Gideon. Luke." Wes extended his hand to both men.

"Mr. Hayes," replied Gideon as he shook Wes's hand.

Luke took the proffered hand without a word.

Wes glanced back to Emma and then her brothers. "Miss Emma, would you mind giving me a private moment with your brothers?"

She opened her mouth to protest, but Gideon cut her off before she could even speak. "Yes, thank you, Emma."

She hadn't planned on staying in the first place, but it still galled her to be sent from the room like a child. Emma gave all three men a final, haughty look then swept out the heavy door not fully closing behind her.

Outside the library, she sagged against the wall. She let

out a deep breath as she mentally reviewed the last several minutes.

What on earth was going on?

One moment, Wes is riding in, looking like the hero of some dime novel at the general store, the next he's acting like he's one of her brothers.

And that touch!

It had been ever so brief, but her ear was still tingling from where his fingertips had grazed her skin. It was a simple act, but it was the most intimate that Emma had ever experienced. Emma finally realized what it was that made women swoon; she'd almost done so herself. And here she had been blaming it all on those awful corsets!

Caught up in the chaos of her mind and body, Emma almost missed overhearing the voices from the library.

"Ah, deputy US marshal, is it? I am guessing our sister does not know." It was Gideon who was speaking.

"Correct. I thought it would be—"

The door was pushed shut from the inside, locking in their words with the thick walls and solid door and sealing in their secrets.

Deputy US marshal!

Weston Hayes was a lawman? What did that mean, and what was his business at the Double H?

She had been so wrapped up in making her point about women earlier, and then experiencing that exhilarating moment between them, that it was only now that Emma realized that Mr. Ha...no, *Deputy US Marshal* Hayes hadn't answered a single one of her questions. She wasn't sure if that was by design, or simply a by-product of his profession, but the result was the same. Emma had no more answers and far more questions than she'd had after their first meeting.

Wes, the marshal, was turning into even more of a mystery than she had expected. And if there was one thing that Emma loved, it was a mystery. Nora knew her too well. This was exactly the sort of thing that drew Emma in.

Puzzles were great fun, and if this one happened to come in a most handsome package, then so be it. She wouldn't allow that to distract from her mission of discovering the secrets of the marshal.

His teasing smile popped back into her mind as she leaned against the wall. She gently bit her bottom lip and touched her ear again. Merciful heavens, Emma was almost certain she could still smell cinnamon. Enough. The last thing she needed was to be found eavesdropping outside the library door.

Making a point this time to fetch her bonnet, Emma made her way back out to the yard to find Tilly. She had so much to think about.

IT HAD TAKEN a few minutes for Luke to warm up to Wes, but once the air was cleared, Wes hoped the Hart brothers would be amenable to his plan.

When he had stopped back at the jailhouse earlier this morning to see Sheriff Wyley, the old lawman had let him know that he had heard there was a McCarty working out at the Double H Ranch, and that was what had sent Wes in this direction. A second chance to see Emma Hart was not his focus for going to the Double H, but he wasn't going to complain about seeing her again. It had been on the ride out that Wes had begun to hatch a plan regarding the McCartys, and while he believed in making his own luck, he still crossed his fingers that the brothers would be open to his idea.

Gideon was the first to respond after he laid his plan before the two men. "Tell me if I got this right. You want us to hire you on at the Double H as a ruse, your intention being to get close to Billy McCarty?"

"That's right," replied Wes. He could see that the eldest Hart brother wasn't convinced.

"Why don't you just go up and ask him what you wanna know? Why bother with the tricks and such?" asked Luke. "All this being sneaky sounds like a waste of time to me. You want to talk to the kid, just ask him straight up."

Luke was asking a fair question. When the sheriff had told him about a McCarty's presence at the Double H, his first thought had been to do exactly that. He even wondered if the bandit brothers had finally split up. It was unlikely, but Wes never assumed anything.

Pointing to the paper atop the oversized wooden desk, Wes replied to Luke's question. "You said your McCarty isn't one of mine."

"No, these men are much older. Billy is still just a young fella, hardly old enough to shave." Gideon spoke in a measured and considering tone, which Wes was beginning to see reflected the man himself. Gideon didn't rush his decision-making. Wes could respect that.

Wes nodded. "I don't want to scare this kid off. He may know something without even realizing what he knows. If he's any relation to the men I'm after, they may try to contact him." Then Wes added, "If he's not part of their mess already."

"I can't see it," said Luke.

Gideon agreed. "He hasn't been here long, but so far he's

proven himself to be a quick learner and dependable work-er." Gideon turned to his brother. "You hear any different?"

Luke shook his head. "He hasn't even angered any of the boys at the bunkhouse yet, and that's saying some-thing. Even Wilson likes him, and he takes a while to warm up to most folks." He shrugged. "I got no complaints."

Wes watched patiently as Gideon rubbed his fingers back and forth across his forehead. The eldest Hart seemed to be struggling with something.

"You don't have to pay me, if that's your worry. I'll do all the work required. I only ask that you pair me up with McCarty if it's ever possible." Wes hoped his reassurance would assist Gideon in making his decision.

Luke snorted a laugh, and Gideon gave him a quizzical look before replying, "It's not the money."

There was no reason to doubt those words. From the moment he'd crossed into the Hart's land, he could see how well-maintained it was. It was a big outfit, and they seemed to be quite successful. Even as he walked through their home, the few moments he took his eyes off the swaying figure of Emma Hart, he could tell that the Harts had long since stopped worrying about where their next meal would come from. From the talk in town, they were also well-respected.

Was it that they didn't think it was their problem? That if it didn't affect their business, then it wasn't their concern?

"I know these aren't hanging offenses, but aren't you tired of men thinking they can get away with these kinds of behaviors? Do you really want men like that around Autumn Springs? Did you read how long that list is?" Wes again pointed to the paper on the desk.

Gideon sighed and nodded, but Luke was suddenly livid

at the question. "I read it just fine. You think I couldn—didn't! 'Course I did ... we both did."

Wes noticed the silent exchange between the brothers and then Luke was once again silent. He had no idea what that was about, but he knew better than to ask. He was already on thin ice with Luke; he didn't need to irritate him further.

"Then what's your concern, Gideon?"

"I guess it feels a little underhanded to me. Billy hasn't done a single thing to warrant this deception. He's not broken our trust, and I prefer to show him the same respect. I'm not sure it's right," explained Gideon.

If he had had any doubts about the character of Gideon Hart, those were dissolved instantly at the man's words. He was a good man, and the reputation that preceded him was well-deserved.

"I can understand feeling that way, and I respect you all the more for it. But the odds are, that boy is related. If his last name was Smith or something more common, I might not even bother, but there can't be that many McCartys in this area that aren't blood."

Gideon nodded with a sigh. "All right."

"It had better be Billy you got your eye on out here and nothing else. Marshal or not, our sister—"

"Luke. I believe the marshal understands and will be focused on his work. He's to find out more about the McCartys and nothing else. That sound about right, Marshal?"

His words were formed as a question, but Gideon's message was as clear as Luke's direct one. Stay clear of their sister. Emma was off limits and that was not up for negotiation. Wes knew he would be expected to treat her with respect, but he had never intended any differently. There was no point in defending himself or trying to reassure them; their point had been made, and it didn't require discussion. If he wanted to stay and make any headway on his McCarty case, then he would be expected to follow their rules.

Wes wasn't about to say no. He needed an in to get Creed and Felix McCarty, and the last thing he needed was more time with Miss Emma Hart. Those last moments they had spent in each other's company had been dangerous enough for him.

It had taken all his strength to pull away from her and fight the urge to capture her sweet lips with his. She was such a mix of sass and sweet that it had him spinning. Being near Emma had made him nearly forget who he was and what he was, and that was something he could never do. Ever.

"Of course," promised Wes.

Pushing back his coat, he removed the metal badge that had been hidden behind. "I'm hoping I can leave this with you. In case anyone gets overly curious about the new guy and starts rummaging through my things."

Gideon took the badge from Wes and placed it inside a drawer in the desk. "I wouldn't expect that, but I understand. The paper too?" he indicated to the writ still on the desk between them.

"I'd be much obliged," said Wes.

Gideon tucked the paper alongside the badge in the drawer and closed it. "You sure you're up for this, Marshal? Working a ranch isn't something I expect you're used to." He smiled. "Fewer bullets, more sweat."

Wes grinned. "We'd better drop the 'Marshal,' for a while. And yes, I think I'll be fine. I've never been afraid of hard work. In some ways, the change will be nice."

Luke laughed, but it wasn't with any malice. "Good. You'll find plenty of that here." He paused and then his eyes brightened. "I reckon if we are dropping the 'Marshal' to keep up appearances, you should start calling me 'Mr. Hart,' going forward."

Wes could see how much Luke was enjoying himself now and couldn't help but chuckle at the suggestion. "That won't be a problem for me...Mr. Hart."

Even Gideon's mouth twitched at the exchange. If Wes hadn't been watching, he would have missed it. He wondered if the solemn man ever fully smiled.

"I think that Luke and Gideon will be just fine, Mar— Wes. We aren't overly formal here at the Double H."

Wes glanced over to Luke and was met with a shrug and a wink. "If big brother says so."

"He does," replied Gideon.

Luke laughed.

For a moment, Wes wondered if this is what it would have been like to have a younger sibling, or any siblings for that matter. Not that it mattered much; he was just glad that Luke was no longer looking to knock him out.

There wasn't much left to discuss and the sooner he met young Billy McCarty, the better. He needed to bring in Felix and Creed before they caused any further harm.

"Well, I guess I'd better get started," Wes declared.

"Luke," said Gideon. "Why don't you take Wes out to the bunkhouse, so he can meet some of the fellas that are here. Have him and McCarty on the old corral tomorrow. It needs some work, and the two of them can do it together. It will allow time for talk."

Gideon still looked pained. "We'll have you and Billy together for most work if we can, without making it too obvious. Hopefully that can speed up this whole thing. I really don't like doing this to the kid. He said he came here for a fresh start, and that's what I want him to have."

Luke and Wes left Gideon in the library and made their way to the bunkhouse. It wasn't close to the main house but was still too short a distance to ride. He took the opportunity to ask Luke about their operation. It was an impressive spread. Mountains off to the south, rolling hills and abundant pasture in every other direction; the Harts had found a good place to lay claim. Their main business was cattle, but another Hart brother, Ben, had been thinking of expanding into horseflesh, as the army was in constant need of mounts. With hogs, chickens, and a menagerie of other animals, Wes asked why there were no sheep in evidence on Double H property. Luke scoffed at the idea that any respectable rancher would raise sheep. Wes wasn't sure he agreed but thought it best to keep his opinion to himself, seeing as he and Luke were finally getting on.

The yard and outbuildings were attended to with the same care the main house received. When Luke told him that Double H had started up over two decades ago, he expected to see at least a few weathered and beaten barns; perhaps some leaning fence and pens. But the gardens looked tended and other than an axe lodged in a splitting stump, there were no tools or farm implements left out. A small cabin was visible from the big house, and while it didn't appear lived in, it wasn't in disrepair. The only thing that dared to stray from its place was an occasional tumbleweed drifting through the yard. The Harts obviously took pride in their home, and there was no doubt about how much Luke loved the land he was working on.

Wes wondered if he could have that same connection to a piece of dirt. There was something to be said for having your own place in the world. Something to build and to pass on. Not that he had anyone to pass anything on to. That wasn't in the cards for him.

He'd never thought he would do anything differently from the work his own father had chosen. It had come at a harsh cost, but Wes had never known anything different. He couldn't even picture himself doing anything else. He believed in the law and Justice and was proud of his part to see that it was carried out, but he didn't have a passion for it. Not the kind that Luke had in his voice when he talked about the Double H.

Wes couldn't imagine ever loving anything that much. The closest he came was with Bass, his horse. But somehow, Wes didn't think that was quite the same thing.

A flashing pair of deep brown eyes, with a thick fringe of lashes to match, popped into his mind. Wes quickly pushed the image away. Where had that come from?

He looked to Luke to make sure the man had not read his mind, then glanced back at the main house. He needed to get a hold of himself. He had work to do, and a promise to keep.

5

Emma had barely begun her meal, but it seemed that all four of her brothers were already halfway through their plates. Not that she could blame them. Her brothers worked hard, and hard-working men need to fill their bellies. It didn't hurt that Teresa La Baena was an amazing cook. Teresa often pondered out loud if they had ever been full.

She pushed another gravy-coated piece of potato around her plate, trying to figure out how to ask about Deputy US Marshal Weston Hayes without arousing her brothers' suspicions. Emma couldn't believe that he hadn't told her he was a marshal. It made no sense to her why he should with-hold that information when they had first met. A simple, "I'm Marshal Hayes, pleased to meet you" would not have been complicated. What was he up to? She hated being kept in the dark. She was twenty-one years old, an adult, not some child who couldn't be trusted with the truth.

"Are you planning on eating that spud, or are you going to keep playing with it?" asked Ben.

Before she could even answer, he'd speared it with his fork and popped it into his mouth, grinning. Tilly giggled at her uncle's antics and Emma tried to give her most good-natured brother a scathing look, failing miserably. It was impossible to be irritated by Ben.

She decided instead to use his thieving of her food to her advantage. "I see you're awfully hungry. You must be working much harder these days. Is that why we have hired on Mr. Hayes?"

Emma watched as her words led to an almost comical chain reaction of glances between her brothers, and she inwardly sighed. Did they really believe her to be that obtuse? It was obvious that Luke and Gideon had let Ben and Rhett in on whatever it was that was going on. She tried, unsuccessfully, not to be upset that they hadn't thought to trust her as well. Emma wouldn't be surprised if a telegram had already been sent to Micah to apprise him of the situation. Heaven forbid a Hart be left out. A male one anyway.

It was Gideon who answered. "A little extra help, nothing more."

Luke looked across the table at Ben. "Can't say I've ever seen a time when Ben hasn't been...what did you say, Emma? 'Awfully hungry.'"

The whole table laughed at the accuracy of Luke's words, including Ben, who took the teasing in stride.

The Harts were all tall, solid, dark-haired men, but Ben carried a few pounds more than the others. Emma doubted there was much more than a pinch of fat on him; he'd just always been *big* for as long as she could remember. Rhett used to say that Ben was too big to ride and too small to hitch a wagon to. The size of him could scare some folks off, but Emma knew that Ben's heart was as big as he was.

He shrugged at Luke's teasing, and said, "A man's gotta eat!" Then he swiftly impaled the carrots that Tilly had been avoiding on her plate and deposited them in his mouth with a wink to his niece.

Tilly covered her mouth as she giggled at her uncle's sneaky assistance and whispered a thank you. She then turned to Gideon. "Daddy, I can be extra help. I'm getting real strong."

Emma watched Gideon smile warmly at his daughter. Tilly was one of the few things that could bring the light back into his eyes. "'Course you can, honey. You've been a big help around here. Teresa was just saying that very thing the other day."

Tilly beamed.

"The thing is, I need to hire men so that you can still focus on your learning."

"I learn lots from Early and Lee Manning. They's been—"

"They've," corrected Gideon.

"They...s been learning me lots of good stuff."

Emma and Tilly's three uncles were desperately trying to hold in their laughter. The 'good stuff' that Tilly was claiming to have learned from the ranch hands of the Double H would have absolutely mortified Tilly's poor departed mother. Cordelia had been a lady through and through.

Gideon cleared his throat and replied to his daughter. "I meant ladylike learning, Matilda."

"That's boring," declared Tilly, her nose wrinkling. It was obvious she thought as highly about ladylike learning as she did cooked carrots.

"That's appropriate," replied Gideon.

Emma hesitated, then spoke. "Gideon have you ever thought that—"

"No. The topic is not open for discussion, Emma." He looked around the table. "From any of you."

Her brother's wife had passed away in an accident two years before and he refused to even enter a conversation about remarrying. Emma knew that and had no intention of speaking of it in front of Tilly.

"If you had let me finish, I was going to say: have you reconsidered my mention of a nanny?"

"I don't need a nanny. Those are for babies," interrupted Tilly.

Emma looked down the table at Tilly. "You're right. A governess then. Someone who can devote themselves—"

"I have you and Teresa. And Tilly will be at school soon, too," sighed Gideon.

He wasn't even going to let her finish her sentences. "You know what I mean."

Rhett cleared his throat loudly and glared at both her and Gideon while giving a subtle nod to Tilly.

"We can discuss this another time, Emma," said Gideon.

Emma looked to Luke and Ben for support, but both men avoided her eyes. Cowards. It was always another time, which in Gideon's world meant never.

Emma didn't bother to pursue it. Like with the marshal, she would have to find answers and a solution by herself.

After supper, Emma read a story to Tilly, and then Gideon came out from his office, to put his daughter to bed. It was a ritual that had begun when Cordelia had passed, and they two of them had moved back into the big house. It gave Emma hope that Gideon's heart hadn't been closed off completely. He mouthed the words 'thank you' to Emma as he carried Tilly off to her room. How could she stay angry with him? He was doing the best he could. His world had been turned upside down, and he was still here, still loving Tilly and still a part of this family. Who knows how she would have handled it all, had she been in Gideon's shoes?

After finishing off a few more chapters in the book she was reading for her own pleasure, Emma headed to her own room and prepared for bed. Opening the window, she let the cool night air wash over her. In the distance, she could see the glow from the bunkhouse campfire, and a hint of male laughter floated across the expanse between the two buildings.

It was too far away to make out Wes's form, but that didn't stop Emma from imagining him there. She wondered what he was up to. Whatever it was, it had to be more exciting than the day in and day out of her life.

Emma tamped down any lingering frustration she had with Gideon. She loved sweet Tilly to bits and wished, one day, for children of her own, just like her niece; but there was a part of her that didn't think it was fair to expect her or Teresa to give up their lives because he refused to go on living his.

Guilt filled her at the selfish direction of her thoughts. She was being awful. She was so blessed, the last thing she should be doing was feeling sorry for herself. Her family needed her and that's where her responsibility lay. Gideon hadn't complained when he'd been forced to take over as head of the family after their parents died. She needed to chin up and return that kindness.

Still, responsibilities or not, her curiosity about Wes wouldn't harm anyone. She wasn't going to do anything that would harm her reputation, that wasn't even a concern. The distraction provided by his arrival at the Double H was just the thing she needed, and it had nothing to do with the twinkle in his blue eyes as he teased her, or the way being near him made her heart beat faster. She was almost sure of it.

In fact, she should stop being vexed by her brothers and instead be thanking them. If they had explained the reason for Wes's presence at the Double H, she would have no mystery to solve. Without realizing it, her brothers had actually made her days significantly more interesting.

Stepping away from the window, Emma closed the curtains before she slipped into bed. Her toes wiggled with the excitement of the next day. One way or another, she was going to find out why Deputy US Marshal Weston Hayes was working at the Double H ranch.

The Pinkertons would have nothing on her. If she couldn't get Wes to confess, then she would do a little investigating all on her own.

~

SETTLING into the bunkhouse had been a smooth process. Wes was impressed by the accommodations. They were far better than any bunkhouse he'd seen before, and better than many places (claiming to be hotels) where he'd stayed. It was comfortable and certainly cleaner.

Word from the men was that the Harts were a good family, and the Double H was one of the best outfits to be working for. They treated their employees fairly and didn't give anyone cause for complaint.

He had briefly met Mendo La Baena, the foreman, who had been out earlier with Ben and Rhett Hart. With his calm demeanor, and friendly treatment of the hands, Wes could see why the ranch hands respected him. Although he worked along side the men, Mendo didn't stay in the bunkhouse. He had his own place nearby with his wife Teresa. The La Baenas had been very close to the Harts' parents and had been with them since they first came to the area.

He met all the workers available. Some were still out at the boundary cabins and would be back in a few days. Young Billy McCarty had introduced himself and then begged off, hitting the sack instead of joining the others. He seemed friendly enough, just worn out from another day's work.

Soon Wes found himself by a fire, sitting next to a hand called Early. He was a slim, older, dark man with a lifetime of wrinkles around his smiling eyes. A heavy-lidded, haggard-looking fella named Wilson Booker was on the other side. Across from him was a light-blond cowboy as tall as Wes, with long legs that stretched out toward the fire. He'd introduced himself as Lee Manning, and the other boys seemed to use his full name each time they addressed him. The last man to join them at the fire was Virgil Lamb. He was sporting a fine-looking mustache that he obviously took much pride in, as he was constantly twirling and smoothing it down. The boys kept calling him 'Glory' and when Wes asked how he got the nickname, it was Lee Manning who spoke up to quip that Glory spent more time with his nose in the Bible than his back end sat a horse.

Wes found himself enjoying the company and appreciating the back-and-forth the hands were giving each other. Having been an only child and now working in a profession that could leave him on his own for weeks at time, it was nice to be around the good-humored group.

Lee Manning questioned him first. Wes was surprised it

had taken them this long to dig a little deeper than an introduction of names.

"So, what brings you to the Double H, Weston Hayes?" drawled Lee Manning.

"'Wes' will do fine. I needed work." He didn't want to create a complicated story that could come back to bite him. It also didn't feel right lying to a group of people who'd done nothing but treat him fairly thus far. It was a hazard of his job. Sometimes he needed to do things that made folks uncomfortable, and there were other times that merely confessing to being a lawman could get you spat on. It wasn't always easy, but Wes was still proud of the work he did. While not everyone understood what it took, he knew he was doing his part in making life better for folks. He still didn't like lying. He was enjoying his time with the Double H ranch hands, and he hoped that when the time came, they would understand why he'd had to do what he'd done.

"Didn't know they was hiring," commented Booker from beside Wes. Booker's gaze never left the fire as he spoke. "Mendo ain't said nothin'."

"Guess I got lucky," Wes shrugged. "It was Gideon and Luke that brought me on."

Of all the men, Booker was the least friendly, although he hadn't been unpleasant. Not everyone was up to being buddies with a stranger. If their positions were switched, Wes would have been reserved with a new man too.

"You complaining about an extra set of hands around here, Booker?" asked Early.

Booker spat a stream of tobacco into the fire with obvious expertise. "Wouldn't do that. I's just saying."

"Where are you from, Wes?" Glory had decided to ask a few questions of his own. "You been wrangling long? No disrespect intended, but you don't have the weary look of a cowpoke I'm used to." Glory laughed at his own words. "Guess I'm only disrespecting the rest of us."

Wes smiled. "I'll confess, I'm not as wedded to the life as you boys. I've been working different jobs from town to town. Always looking." He wasn't lying; he was only leaving out what it was he was looking for. Or, rather, who he spent his days looking for.

"Looking for what?" Glory pushed.

Wes shrugged again. "Changes all the time."

"Now, now," Early soothed. "How about we save the questions for another time? Not every man wants to share his business."

What could only be described as a grunt came from Booker at Early's remark. Wes hoped he hadn't alienated the men with his evasive answers. It was a fine line to walk between lying straight-out and playing his cards close.

It was also a good reminder that, as the new man at the Double H, he would likely be under more scrutiny and observation until he proved himself trustworthy. Wes needed to remember that if he and Emma crossed paths around the ranch. If he didn't keep his mind on the tasks he was assigned and his own mission, he had a feeling that these friendly fellas would have him regretting his choices. He was going to need to think of Emma as just another Hart, like one of the boys.

The soft lips that had been so close to his earlier in the day appeared in his mind. Wes berated himself for his momentary lack of control. He was lucky that they hadn't been seen, and that he had somehow found the strength to pull away. What had he been thinking? Miss Emma Hart was never going to be 'one of the boys.' He needed to keep his mouth shut, head down, and eyes on the prize. And, despite his wayward thoughts, that prize was never going to be Emma.

The rest of the evening, Wes spent his time listening to the conversation, learning more about the Hart brothers and the scope of their operation. He also discovered that there had been some cattle missing lately and while there weren't enough missing to alert Sheriff Wyley back in Autumn Springs, the ranch hands were keeping a close watch. These men took pride in their work, and the fact that someone or something had been stealing from the Harts was no different than if it had been taken from the wranglers' own pockets. There was some talk that it might be someone from the Lafferty Ranch, out to the east of the Double H, but there was no consensus or proof. Apparently, there was a good-natured rivalry between the two ranches, but cattle-rustling was no laughing matter, and Early didn't think the Laffertys were dishonest men.

As a marshal, Wes was tasked with tracking down the McCartys and bringing them to justice. Cattle-rustling wasn't in his purview, but if he had the opportunity to look into the matter of the missing animals, he would. The Harts had been decent to him and helpful when they weren't required to be. He hoped he would be able to return the favor.

Slowly, each hand drifted away from the fire and headed to bed. Morning wasn't far away, and sleep was needed. He was going to be working with young Billy McCarty tomorrow, so he also needed to get some shuteye. Wes wondered if the boy would be a help, or if this entire ruse was a waste of time. He would know soon enough. If Billy was no relation to the outlaws, then Wes needed to move on; not only to continue his search for the McCarty brothers, but to get himself clear of the intriguing Emma Hart.

The image of her face was coming to mind so often he was starting to worry that he might be in danger of losing more than just the McCartys. A woman like Emma could easily steal a man's heart, and Wes knew that he couldn't let that happen. The cost was too high.

6

The sun had barely cleared the horizon as Emma and Tilly made their way to the milking barn. It was one of Emma's favorite times, when the world was just waking up to the promise of a new day. Even the air seemed fresher.

As much as she craved the opportunity to see more of the world, Emma loved her home at the Double H Ranch. With an operation as large as theirs, there were many moving parts to maintain in order to keep it running smoothly. No two days were ever the same. Emma loved that.

The ranch hands handled the milking, but this morning Emma and Tilly were going to grab a bucket of creamy milk before it got too busy. They had been in the kitchen when Teresa mentioned she would be making more butter today.

Teresa's plans provided an excellent opportunity for Tilly to fully understand the process from beginning to end. Everyone enjoyed a thick slice of Teresa's freshly made bread, slathered in butter, but it was important for Tilly to know where her food was coming from and how it was made. Tilly's excitement about every aspect of ranch life made her a treat to look after. Emma often found herself caught up in her niece's delight, as did many of the workers. Not having her mother at her side was tough for a girl at any age, and Emma was grateful for the abundance of love that Tilly received from everyone on the Double H.

Entering the barn hand in hand, Tilly and Emma quickly realized that they weren't the first ones in the stalls this morning. There was a soft whistling coming from their right. Holding a finger to her lips, Emma smiled mischievously at Tilly, tilting her head to better hear the low voice from within. Whoever it was, was talking in a gentle, soothing voice to the cow in the stall. Emma didn't hold much with gambling, but if she were forced to make a bet, her money would be on the voice belonging to Wes.

They crept closer to see if they could make out what he was saying to the creature in front of him.

"See that, Bessie? To think you doubted me, even for a minute. I only needed a reminder, and that tail of yours was more than enough. Look what a fine team we make now. And the fellas in the bunkhouse thought I wouldn't be able to get this done. Thankfully, I passed their first test. We'll see how I fare as the day moves along."

Tilly covered her smile with a hand, but her sparkling eyes declared what a grand bit of fun she was having. Emma was thinking the same when she realized her behavior was entirely the wrong example to be setting for her niece. Her belief that she was always about to miss out on something had led to the terribly rude habit of eavesdropping on her brothers. She had been doing it so long that she often forgot how ill-mannered it really was.

Perhaps if she confessed her habit to Gideon, that would

be enough to convince him that his daughter needed a proper governess.

Straightening her back, Emma peeked around the stall to let Wes know she and Tilly were there.

"Good morning, Mr. Hayes. I see you've made a new friend."

Both man and bovine turned their heads at the early-morning intrusion. "Miss Emma, dare I ask how long you've been standing there?"

Emma had the decency to blush at his words.

"And Miss Tilly! Is that you I see there?" He shot a wide grin at her niece, which was instantly returned.

"Yup, it's me," announced Tilly, and she walked right up to Wes. The little girl was practically breathing down his neck, she was standing so close.

Wes continued to fill the milk bucket below. Emma wanted to ask him a thousand questions, but none were suitable while Tilly was present. Whatever business Wes, the marshal, had here, it was not likely to involve the little girl.

Instead, it was Tilly who started interrogating Wes.

"How did you know her name is Bessie?" Emma watched as her niece stuck her face directly in front of Wes's while she spoke, ensuring she had the man's full attention.

To his credit, Wes seemed unaffected by the girl's bold nature.

"How did I know?" said Wes. "Why Bessie told me herself, of course!"

Tilly looked to the cow and then back to Wes. "Cows don't do that."

"Do what? Tell you their names?" asked Wes, his face absolutely serious as he spoke. "How do you know?"

Tilly turned back to Emma, looking for support. It was

hard for Emma to keep the twitch of her lips from turning into a smile. She was curious to see how this entire exchange would play out.

"I just do," stated Tilly, with five-year-old conviction.

Wes gave the girl a doubtful frown. "Have you ever asked one what its name was before, or do you just go around naming cows what you like all willy-nilly?"

Emma choked down her threatening laughter. What was it about a man who was good with children that made him doubly attractive? She still had no idea who Marshal Weston Hayes really was or if he was anywhere near an acceptable suitor, but he was well on his way to checking off all the boxes that mattered to her.

Tilly shook her head. "No."

"Well then." He stopped milking the cow potentially known as Bessie, to throw up his hands. "There you have it. There's only one way to prove it."

"How?" Tilly still seemed rather skeptical, but Emma could tell that the little girl was being pulled in by the tall tale.

"Simple," said Wes. He motioned to the front of the stall, where the cow was lazily chewing. "You ask her."

Tilly eyed Wes and then looked over to Emma. Emma only shrugged. Walking behind the marshal on the low stool, Tilly went right up to the cow's large head.

"What's your name? Is it really Bessie?" whispered the girl.

The cow began a gentle lowing and then stopped with a snort into the air between her and the girl.

"See! Bessie. I told you," Wes affirmed.

"That's not talkin' at all," declared Tilly with a scowl.

"Sure, it is. I guess you just don't speak bovine, yet." Wes shrugged and went back to milking Bessie.

"You're foolin' me. I can tell. Auntie Emma, you tell him."

Crossing her arms and leaning against the entrance of the stall, Emma agreed with her niece. "I'm with Tilly, Mr. Hayes. I didn't hear it either."

Wes shook his head in mock disgust. "You're telling me neither of you speak bovine? And both of you born and raised on a ranch. Boy, oh boy, I never."

He sent a wink towards Emma that made her tingle straight through to her fingertips, and then a well-placed steam of milk that hit squarely on the tops of Tilly's bare feet, which were peeking out from beneath the hem of her dress, and then trickled down between her toes.

The little girl shrieked at the liquid attack and burst into a fit of giggles. Startled by the sound, Bessie bellowed, and Wes took a swift tail to the side of his face as a reprimand.

Emma gasped. "Tilly! Your feet! Where are your shoes?" She looked down at her niece's wiggling wet toes, mixed in with hay and heaven knew what else. "Back to the house with you. Clean off those feet and tell Teresa I will be there momentarily."

Still giggling, Tilly scampered out of the stall and back toward the main house.

Watching her go, Emma said, "Honestly, how that child's feet aren't full of splinters and thorns is beyond understanding." She spun back to Wes. "And you, Mr. Hayes, with your teasing, are no better."

"Don't go blaming me, if you can't understand your own livestock."

His feigned look of innocence was particularly endearing, and Emma felt her heart flutter. He wasn't only the most attractive man she had ever laid eyes on; he was funny too. Another box checked on the list.

"What are you doing out here? Has Mendo assigned you milking duties?" asked Emma.

"No, it was more of a challenge from the boys at the bunkhouse. They didn't think I was up to the task. I'll confess it took a few attempts, but after Bessie and I talked about it, we came to an understanding. I was glad to find I wasn't completely out of practice."

"No, your aim was spot on," laughed Emma. Wes joined her with a chuckle.

"She's a pretty sweet kid. Smart too. Wasn't having none of my nonsense."

Emma could see he was sincere. "She is definitely both of those things. Gideon is lucky to have her. We all are." Wes nodded.

Bucket full, Wes stood and took the few steps to stand before her. As a Hart, Emma was taller than most of the women she knew in Autumn Springs, and many of the men; but standing before Wes, she felt rather delicate. Her brothers were all tall too, but she had never given it a second thought when standing next to them. The marshal was just so, so very manly. Even his jawline seemed to be carved from granite.

"Were you in need of some milk?"

Emma wasn't sure what she was in need of anymore; the nearness of Wes had her upside down and backwards. "Pardon me?"

"The milk." Wes held up the bucket. "Was that what you two came to the barn for?"

Embarrassed she had been caught daydreaming; Emma felt the heat flood her cheeks. "Yes. Yes, of course. Teresa, Tilly, and I will be making butter today, and I thought I would have Tilly see the undertaking from beginning to end."

"Then you'd better take this." Wes held out the bucket.

"Right. Thank you." Emma smiled. "I'll be sure to send some over to Stink at the bunkhouse. I hope you haven't been put off by his name. I assure you his cooking is top-notch!"

Laughing, she moved to take the bucket from Wes, their bare hands touching in the exchange.

They both went completely still.

If lightning had struck her down then and there, Emma was sure it would have felt the same. Less pain, but the same amount of heat. As her eyes widened with the contact, she saw in his eyes that he felt it too. In that moment, Emma knew that there was something special between them, and though she couldn't put it into words or explain it, it was the most real and exciting thing she had ever experienced.

Her heart hammered in her chest, and she wondered if he could hear the sound of it. For a moment, she couldn't speak. Even if she could have, she would not have trusted herself to. Then, as her eyes searched his, she saw a change, as though a curtain fell across his gaze. He released her fingers.

She almost dropped the bucket, their disconnect was so abrupt.

What had happened? Was it something she had done? All of this was so new to her that Emma didn't know up from down.

"Sorry. I mean, thank you," Emma mumbled. She was so confused. What had caused Wes to shut down as he had?

"You're welcome, Miss Hart. Do you need any assistance getting the bucket back, or should I take it over for you?"

Miss Hart. Not Miss Emma. What was going through his mind? She had so many questions about what had taken place between them, but it was obvious that he was not interested in reviewing it with her. She needed to put it aside for the moment and move on. There would be a time to deal with this new feeling, but that time was not now.

Emma took a deep breath, shaking off the thrill and confusion of their exchange.

She didn't want to walk away quite yet, and after brief contemplation, Emma decided that having him carry the milk for her might give her a chance to ask a few more questions. She wasn't going to worry if he thought her fragile for not carrying it on her own. Now she had a greater priority.

"Yes, please."

She wondered if he recognized that for most of the young ranch hands on the Double H, this would be the end of their conversation. It didn't matter, not really. Emma still wanted to speak to Wes, and she knew, even if he didn't realize that she did, that he was no ranch hand.

Emma was curious as to what it would take to make him confess his secret to her. To admit that he was actually a marshal and not a wrangler. She was dying to know why a deputy US marshal was pretending to be a cowhand. To his credit, he didn't seem out of place. He must have had at least some farm experience, if not on a ranch, because so far, he was playing his part quite well.

"What kind of work did you do at the last ranch you were at?" asked Emma.

When he gave her an odd look, she wasn't sure if it was the sudden change of topic or the question itself that made him eye her the way he was. He had never really said that he had been at another ranch prior to the Double H; could he see through to her intentions?

"I've done a bit of everything, it seems. It's often different from week to week, at times day to day."

She felt a grudging surge of appreciation at his clever response. Had she not known he was a marshal, he would have sounded very much like a drifter who had no ties to anyone or anything, and no real plans. But she did know who, or at least what, he was. His answer wasn't an outright lie, but it was definitely evasive.

The idea that Wes would cave in and confess all after just one question had been silly. After all, he was probably a professional at interrogation himself. It shouldn't be a surprise that he could so easily dodge her efforts to do so.

"That way of life doesn't bother you? You don't mind having no plans or direction?" Normally Emma would never be so rude as to ask such a question, but Wes was playing a game, and she didn't feel bad about joining in. "I can't imagine what it must be like to never really *go after* something. To let things fall into my lap instead of *investigating* my passions. I could never *justice-fy* living so *lawlessly*, to myself."

Wes looked at her like she might be touched in the head. Emma thought she was being quite clever, but perhaps her expertise in innuendo was lacking. She had wanted to hint to Wes that she knew he was a marshal, but she didn't want to say it outright. Emma preferred he simply come clean and tell her the truth.

"I'm not exactly sure what you meant by all that, but I feel like you may have just insulted me," said Wes.

A few minutes ago, Wes had been losing himself in the soft fingers that had touched his and cursing his lack of control when it came to all things Emma Hart; now he was speculating that somewhere between here and the touch at the milking barn that had sent them both reeling Emma had lost her mind. Only half of what she'd just said made any sense.

"That wasn't my intention. I was responding to your own description of your life."

That was fair. He was being misleading, and what he had given her made him sound like a ne'er-do-well who was without goals and never thought about a future. For someone like Emma, that must be confusing. He was amazed she hadn't grabbed the bucket from his hand and bolted back to the main house, leaving this shiftless drifter behind.

"Fair enough." Wes should have left it there, but he kept talking. "Guess we're different people. You in the big house, folks like me in the bunkhouse."

"That's unwarranted, Mr. Hayes. I don't believe in that kind of thinking, and I didn't think my actions had shown differently. But perhaps you're right, and we are a different sort of people," replied Emma.

Maybe it was better this way. If Emma thought he was just another transient worker passing through the Double H, that might be for the best. They didn't need any more moments like the one they'd shared in the barn.

The touch of her fingertips on his had awakened something in him that was best left buried. Emma had sparked a fire in him that needed to be extinguished before it burned them both up. He doubted she even realized the need she had stirred in him. It was obvious that she had felt the attraction too, but Emma was too innocent to understand the depths of its meaning.

Wes knew, and it scared him.

He had accepted long ago that his life would take a

certain path. Contrary to what he had said to Emma, Wes knew exactly what direction he was headed in. He had learned from his past and knew that he would never invite such danger and pain into his life again.

Emma was a lightness that he could never have, and that was all there was to it. She was a lady, and she deserved more than he could ever offer. It didn't matter that even being near her was enough to make him question his entire life. It was what it was.

He needed to stop making excuses to be near her. He needed to keep his mind on his job and keep his promise to Gideon and Luke. The picture of Emma at his side needed to be wiped from his thoughts. It wasn't going to happen. It couldn't.

They walked the rest of the way in silence. Wes made sure to leave enough space between them that there could be no accidental brushing of their bodies. He couldn't be sure that his heart wouldn't overrule his mind for control of his body. He was having a hard enough time keeping his eyes straight ahead instead of looking over at her. Wes hadn't even known that there were that many shades of brown. He'd always figured hair was hair, until now. He wished she'd worn a bonnet this morning, because watching the rays of the morning sun touch her tresses made him desperate to do the same.

Wes walked a little faster.

She probably thought he was being bad-tempered. He knew that he had hurt her feelings, and as bad as he felt, it couldn't be helped. There was a connection between them that neither one of them could deny with any honesty, and he didn't want to let her think it might be worth pursuing.

If she thought he was a rude rolling stone, then he

needed to let her continue to think that way. It was better for them both.

After leaving both Emma and the milk at the main house, Wes headed back to the bunkhouse to meet up with Billy McCarty. He hoped that his day would include a never-ending supply of punishing work. It was the only thing that was going to chase Emma from his mind.

7

S itting outside on the porch at Nora's, Emma thought about the last few days. She'd gone through a range of emotions that would surely have exhausted an actress walking the boards. Frustration with her attempts to engage Wes in anything more than a perfunctory greeting, which had all been met with failure. It was appearing more and more like deliberate avoidance. There were moments when she could see the teasing rogue who had charmed her at the mercantile. Then the next moment, he'd drop in place a solemn expression and interact in only the most correct of manners.

If people insisted on claiming that women's emotions fluctuated from one moment to the next, then Emma would love to introduce them to the mercurial marshal. Wes was so confusing at times; she couldn't tell if he was coming or going.

Wes went from flashing that brilliant white smile at the mere sight of her, to sending a scowl her way the next. Emma was beginning to wonder if there really was a connection between them, or if it was only in her mind. She had been so certain his flirting and teasing meant he was interested. Had she been so wrong?

There was no reason for him to be afraid of her brothers. He appeared as big and strong as they were, and it wasn't as though he were an honest-to-goodness hired hand of the Double H. He didn't need their pay.

So, what was his problem?

Emma hadn't been asking him to court her; she only wanted a conversation.

She'd wanted to stay bothered by Wes's behavior, but it hadn't taken her long to realize she was being ridiculous. Her questions, followed by that silly attempt to get him to confess his true identity had been a disaster. The fault was hers. Also, she had no idea what his mission was, so she didn't know what kind of pressures he faced. Emma thought that giving him some breathing room might help.

She managed to stay out of his way for a couple of days, but it hadn't stopped her from keeping an eye on him. She never caught him at it but it often felt like his eyes followed her too. Wes hadn't been sent out with the men to check and watch over their herd, which was spread across the wide expanse of the Double H. He spent more of his time with work closer to the main house, outbuildings, and corrals.

Wes was often partnered with Billy McCarty. Emma didn't know too much about the young man, except that he blushed a lot in her company and that, despite only having been at the Double H for a few months, he was well-liked and seemed to get along with the other men. Her brother Ben said that "if he can get Wilson Booker to crack a smile and take him under his wing, then the kid must be a keeper." What made it even more curious, was that her brothers —or was it Mendo? —kept assigning Wes and Billy their work together. Was Billy the reason Wes was here? Emma couldn't imagine what on earth for. Since Billy was younger than she was, she couldn't picture him having had the time to live enough to warrant the attentions of a deputy US marshal. But then again, men were often allowed to live far more exciting lives than women.

Now, watching the two men setting up a new border for Nora's garden, Emma mentally thanked her brother Luke. If her brother had known her innermost thoughts, she doubted that he would ever have sent Wes and Billy to Nora's.

Over breakfast, Emma had casually mentioned how Nora was looking to hire a man from town to come out and fix up her disheveled garden, but that it was so hard to know which men to trust, since they were just two women out there, all by themselves. Luke's gallant nature, and friendship with Nora, had him reacting exactly as Emma planned. He had his own work to do at home, but immediately sent Wes and Billy to perform the work that Nora needed. Emma was fully aware of the deviousness of her plan, but it was still a plan where everyone was a winner.

Nora returned from inside the house, where she had been helping her mother into bed and smiled over at Emma as she sat down in a chair, and continued to shell the peas between them.

"You know you didn't have to send anyone over. I would have gotten to the garden eventually."

Ever since Nora had lost her father and brother to fever, the Harts had been happy to lend assistance to her and her mother in any way required. Rhett, and Nora's brother Nate had been best friends. Both boys had gotten sick, and only Rhett had survived. The devastating loss had been felt by both families.

"You shouldn't have to, Nora. You already do the work of

two men to keep this place going. Besides, I absolutely did. With Tilly making donuts and pie with Teresa today, my actions are not so much benevolent, and far more selfish." Emma returned her best friend's smile.

Nora gave Emma's toe a little nudge with her own. "I had a feeling this might be more for you than me. Although, you won't hear me complaining."

Both women watched the men working away in the garden as Nora spoke quietly. "So, this is your man with the sweet tooth. He's certainly a tall drink of water, I'll say that much. Not that your own brothers aren't walking trees. I swear I don't know what Teresa puts in their food, but it must contain some magic potion."

Emma groaned. "Don't say that! I'm eating the same fare. I'm already as tall as half the men in town. It's no wonder I'm lacking suitors."

"Ha! I can guarantee that your height has nothing to do with it. If you wanted, you could have half the town lined up at your door. You're a beauty just like your mama was. I'd chalk it up to your disinterest and this town's—"

"*Limited* decent prospects," Emma finished for her.

Both girls dissolved into laughter, causing the two men in the garden to raise their heads from their work to see the source of the noise. Emma and Nora both waved. The men quickly resumed, bemused by the ladies' mirth.

"I mean it," declared Nora. "The only decent men, for miles around, are your brothers. And they are like brothers to me, so that doesn't help a thing."

"Not all of them," winked Emma.

Nora blushed. "Stop it. Don't even start."

"With Micah coming home soon, you may find your prospects improved considerably."

Emma's brow furrowed as Nora waved away her words.

"It's been a long time since Micah and I have seen each other, Emma. Things change."

"Not that much, and it hasn't been that long. He's been home for the holidays. Nora, you and Micah were close from the moment you met. You are meant to be together. We all know it. What has you so melancholy?"

Nora stared down at her hands. She let out a slow sigh before she looked back to Emma.

"He stopped writing."

"What?"

"Don't make a fuss. It was bound to happen. He's been in the big city for a long time now. The last time I heard from him, he mentioned he was going to be meeting James Fitzpatrick for dinner. Not a word since then. Whatever childhood feelings we might have had are a thing of the past. He made no promises to me, Emma. As I said, people change. Micah has moved on."

"I don't have a satisfactory explanation for his current behavior, but I do know that what Micah felt was more than a childhood crush."

Emma, like all her brothers, knew that Micah had loved Nora long before Micah himself had realized it. There had never been any doubt in their minds, that one day Nora would be a part of their family, not just in their hearts, but on paper too.

"It's all right, Emma. I've got a home to call my own, I've got Mama, and I have you. It's enough."

It wasn't enough. It was nowhere near enough, to what Nora deserved. Micah would be home soon enough, and this whole mess would be sorted out. Emma fully expected that Micah's exciting news was that he had found the perfect ring while he was gone, and he was going to put that ring on Nora's finger and make them real sisters.

After years of friendship, Emma knew how to recognize when Nora was done talking about a given subject, and Emma respected that. She wasn't going to add any further stress to her friend. When Nora was ready, she would let Emma know.

It was time for a change of topic, and Emma knew just the thing.

"Do you think we should offer them some refreshment?" asked Emma. She was relieved when she heard Nora laugh.

"They've only just started!"

Emma let out a dramatic sigh. "I know, you're right. I honestly don't know what's wrong with me. Who am I? I never thought I'd be acting like an infatuated schoolgirl."

"I'll admit this is a new Emma Hart for me, but I don't blame you. I also don't think this business of yours is one-sided. I declare that your Mr. Hayes spends more time shooting glances this way than he does watching that hammer. If he's not careful, he could lose a finger before the day is through."

"You're teasing," said Emma, sneaking a peek at Wes to see if she could catch him herself.

"I am, but that doesn't mean my observations are untrue." Nora said and smiled.

A wide grin spread across Emma's face, and she felt the tingle of excitement spread through her. She wanted to tell Nora what she had discovered about Wes; the fact that he was actually a deputy US marshal and not really an employee of the Double H. If she couldn't say something to her best friend, then who could she talk to?

"Nora, can I tell you something?"

Nora laughed. "Really? I can't recall you ever asking for permission before."

"Oof, some friend you are," Emma huffed. "My point is

that this time it's top secret. You can't tell another soul; I mean it."

"Seriously. You have been saying that to me our whole lives. Have I ever betrayed your confidence? Of course not. Besides, you are the only person I talk to." Nora gestured to the endless horizon. "This is my life."

"I know. You're my very best of friends."

"Not sure what that says, as you only have me," teased Nora. "So, let's hear it."

Emma didn't need to be told twice. "He's a marshal!"

"Who is? Mr. Hayes?"

"Who else?"

"Then why is he working for your family?"

The puzzled look on Nora's face echoed the confusion Emma had been feeling since she'd first heard the information outside the Hart library.

"That's just it. I don't know. I overheard."

"I feel like it was more like eavesdropping," said Nora.

"Overheard," Emma demurred, then added, "this time. Anyway, I'm not sure, but I think it has something to do with the McCarty boy he's working with there."

Emma tilted her head in the direction of Wes and Billy, as though Nora might have missed who she had been referring to.

"But he's so young."

"Young or not, Wes has been joined at the hip to Billy since he arrived."

Raising one eyebrow and smiling at Emma's familiar use of Wes's given name, she replied, "That is strange, but dare I ask what any of this might have to do with you?"

"It doesn't, but I do find it rather interesting."

Nora winced. "Oh no."

"Oh no, what?" asked Emma.

"Oh no, you don't. The last time I saw that look, you were certain that Gideon, Rhett, and Ben had gotten themselves wrapped up in an outlaw gang," Nora reminded her.

"It was an honest mistake. There had been several robberies, and they were acting fishy," said Emma.

"It was a crazy assumption, and looking back, I don't know how you convinced me to go along with you," said Nora.

Emma grinned at the memory. "It was fun though, wasn't it?"

"Right up until we got caught eavesdropping on the barn roof." Nora laughed. "He still won't admit it, but I know it was Luke who took our ladder away."

"Luke and Micah were mad we hadn't included them in our reconnaissance, but Micah didn't want to get you in trouble. Luke, on the other hand, would have left us up there all night," recalled Emma. "Of course, we'll never really know, since Early and Lee Manning brought us down."

"Your father didn't know whether to be more upset with us being on the roof, the ladder having been taken away, or the things we heard 'that young ladies ought not be privy to.'"

Emma almost snorted as she laughed, remembering her brothers' eye-opening conversation and her father's horror at the questions she had asked afterward.

"I don't know how you weren't scared. I was quaking in my boots, standing there in your father's study."

"I was certain I was on to something and not only would my actions be justified, but actually celebrated," giggled Emma. "Poor Papa. I don't think he ever told Mama about that. She never did figure out why the boys kept calling me Tin Star for weeks after."

"And if I remember correctly, you were *disappointed* to find out that your brothers weren't actually bandits."

"Was I?" asked Emma.

Nora rolled her eyes. "My point, dear Emma, is that whatever reason the marshal has for being here does not concern you. I don't have the time to join you on your wild escapades, and I don't want you to get yourself into something you can't get out of."

"Ugh, Nora, you sound like them."

"Who? Your brothers?"

Emma threw up her hands. "All the men in my life."

"Oh, please," scoffed Nora. "That's the farthest thing from the truth. You have more freedom than most woman around."

"They don't let me do even half of what I would like," Emma objected.

Nora nodded. "Because they know exactly who you are, and the messes you get yourself into. Being protected is not the same thing as being a prisoner."

"Well, it feels like it sometimes."

"That, I can relate to," sighed Nora.

Emma suddenly realized how selfish she was acting and hoped her words hadn't hurt her friend.

"Oh, Nora. I'm sorry. I'm sitting here complaining and never once thinking about the obligations that you carry. I do want to experience more than Autumn Springs, but I would do well to remember how lucky I am."

"It's fine. I'd be a liar if I said that I didn't like being dragged along on your adventures ... sometimes. We all have our crosses to bear, and there is no need to compare them." Nora squeezed the hand that Emma extended, then let go. "Besides, mine is not really that heavy. I'm fortunate to have this land, free and clear, and there are times, when I look in her eyes, that I can still see that Mama is in there. I think it will just take a little more time to piece back the fragments of her broken heart. We don't all grieve the same, and I have to respect that."

"And you," said Emma. "You lost a father and brother too."

"Neither of us have escaped the pain of loss, Emma. There are good days and bad days."

Emma nodded, acknowledging the truth of her best friend's words, and waited for her to continue.

"I actually don't believe that time heals all wounds," revealed Nora. "I know they say that. Maybe they think it will give people more hope for the future. I don't know. Maybe it does heal, but it leaves a scar. One that you live with, not move on from. A reminder of who you are and what you have been through."

"That's both heartbreaking and beautiful at the same time," replied Emma. Nora's words struck a chord deep inside of her.

"I am rather melancholy today, aren't I?" smiled Nora. "I need to get back to my usual way of dealing with things."

"And that is?" asked Emma.

"Distraction. And you have certainly brought that today." Nora contemplated the men working under the open blue sky, just out of earshot.

"In that case, why don't we cut into that pie that I brought?" said Emma.

"I suppose you plan on taking a piece to those hard-working men toiling away out there."

Emma stood and replied in her most demure voice. "Seems the decent thing to do."

Emma knew her motives were utterly transparent, but

that was the benefit of having a best friend. She didn't have to feel bad about being exactly who she was.

"You're incorrigible, Emma Hart," declared Nora, but she also got up and followed Emma inside.

WES WAS TRYING TO FOCUS, but his eyes kept straying to Emma. Each time he heard her tinkling laughter float toward him, a warmth spread through his body. The sound had to be one of the most beautiful things he had ever heard. He noticed he wasn't the only one being affected by the women enjoying their visit on the front porch. Billy McCarty was just as bad.

Billy had been nothing but pleasant, but Wes found himself irritated by the man's distraction. Billy had a job to do, and he should be focused on that, not gawking and staring at Emma with his mooncalf eyes. To be fair, he couldn't be sure it was Emma that Billy was staring at, but either way, he should be keeping his eyes to himself.

For days now, he had been staying on task and away from Emma. He'd been working side by side with Billy McCarty and, while he had enjoyed getting to know him, Wes wasn't making any headway on his case. That had been almost as frustrating as not speaking to Emma while she attended to her duties around the Double H.

Billy cleared his throat and looked past Wes, causing him to turn around.

It was a vision no red-blooded man could refuse.

A beautiful woman, carrying a big piece of pie, walking in his direction. Emma's friend Nora may have been carrying a plate of her own, but Wes wouldn't have noticed; his eyes were glued to Emma.

Billy let out a barely audible whistle only Wes could hear, and he almost turned around to thump him upside the head. Lucky for Billy, that would have meant Wes would have to interrupt his own observation of Emma's glorious approach, and that wasn't happening.

"We felt bad, not sharing, especially while you gentlemen are working so hard," said Emma. She bestowed such a bright smile on the two of them that Wes thought she might outshine the sun. He didn't need to look at Billy to know that the young man's face was beet red.

It was young McCarty who managed to get the first words out. After thanking the ladies for the treat, he asked Nora about the bee colonies she kept. Emma's friend offered to show them to Billy, leaving Emma and Wes alone together for the first time in days.

They hadn't left on the best of terms when they last spoke, and while Wes had thought it necessary at the time, he regretted any hurt he may have caused Emma. After a few days of consideration, he had decided he could still be civil, do his job, and keep his heart under lock and key.

"This looks delicious," said Wes, as he took the proffered plate from Emma, careful not to let their fingers touch.

"I can't take the credit. It was all Teresa. I'm merely the delivery girl. Tilly is with her today, helping to make more. I was fortunate that my brother Ben didn't catch me taking an entire pie off the property. Teresa's apple pie and her buñuelos are a family favorite. Ben would probably have come after me and stopped me at gunpoint had I attempted to bring the buñuelos as well."

"I'll keep that in mind, but you'd better tell me what they are, so I don't grab the wrong thing and have another one of your brothers after me," teased Wes. He couldn't help but smile in response to the pinkening of Emma's cheeks at this reference their first meeting, the smattering of freckles across her nose more obvious against the color. She was a bold woman, but she had a softness to her as well. She was a curious mix.

"Buñuelos? They are like a sugary donut. Hmm. That's not an adequate description.... She makes them better than I could ever describe. Like heaven on your tongue," explained Emma, as Wes dove into the truly excellent pie.

It didn't take long to finish the slice, in spite of its generous size. He and Billy hadn't been working long, but Wes's sweet tooth made short work of the pie. He saw that Billy had also finished his and was now cautiously inspecting the bee hives with Nora.

He wiped his face with the back of his hand, smearing a portion of the filling across his cheek. He rubbed at his face and knew by the amusement on Emma's that he was still unsuccessful.

Pulling out his handkerchief, Wes was about to take another go at it when Emma licked her finger and swept it across his cheek, removing the offending food.

Wes stood absolutely still and watched as the pink that had previously graced Emma's cheeks turned a flaming red. Her mouth dropped open, and Wes didn't dare speak, not trusting himself to even move at this point.

"Oh! I'm—I'm so sorry. I don't know why I did that." Emma glanced over her shoulder, checking to see if Nora and Billy had witnessed her indiscretion. Fortunately, they had not. "I am so used to helping Tilly that I just reacted."

He could still feel where Emma had touched him, but he managed to pull himself together in order to respond. He didn't dare share his thoughts; he decided that humor was best to diffuse the situation.

"I was saving that for later. But it's probably better

removed than walking around with it on in this heat, not to mention the bees." He made sure not to let his lips even twitch as he looked directly into Emma's troubled brown eyes. He watched as relief crossed her face, and Wes knew he had picked the right response.

Emma took the plate from his hand and then looked up at him, her dark eyes once again meeting his.

"I'd better go. Let you both get back to work."

She didn't wait for him to respond; she simply turned and walked away.

Wes was telling himself to tear his gaze from the retreating figure of Emma Hart, when he saw her lick the finger that had touched him only moments before. She glanced back, and their eyes met, before they both quickly turned away.

Picking up the post pounder, Wes called for Billy. If he didn't start working himself into a sweat, right now, there was no chance that image was ever going to leave his mind.

8

The work at Nora Bryson's didn't take them as long as expected, but Emma had returned to the Double H hours earlier. He had watched as she departed, riding astride, like a man born to it. He was beginning to see what a complex woman Miss Emma Hart was. She was like no woman he had met before.

Men in his line of work didn't often cross paths with many women. When he saw them, they were usually either married women, or ladies who made their living via any number of questionable activities. So, while his experience wasn't broad, he could still appreciate the unique woman that Emma was.

His lack of time spent in the company of women might be a consequence of his profession, but it was also a set intention. Being a marshal was nothing like owning a shop or a sawmill. Danger wormed its way into all aspects of his life, and that was no place for a lady.

It was that final thought that made him look across to Billy McCarty, riding at his side. He needed to get to business and start finding out what it was that Billy might know.

"Pretty easy day," Wes commented, hoping Billy might start chatting and then Wes could steer the conversation in the direction that he wanted.

"Lucky too. Stink Wheeler makes a decent pie, but they are few and far between, and we ain't never gettin' them at breakfast."

Wes nodded. "I'll take sweets any time of day."

Billy gave him a side glance and opened his mouth and then shut it again, like he might be wanting to say something. Wes waited. Billy would get to it soon enough.

When he finally did, Wes wished he hadn't.

"She likes you."

It was a statement, not a question, and Wes knew he needed to nip any talk like that in the bud.

"I don't know what you're talking about," he replied, hoping that would put an end to it.

Billy only laughed. "That gonna be your story?"

Wes needed to change the subject and quick. The last thing he needed to be discussing with Billy McCarty was what Emma Hart was or was not feeling, even less so his own thoughts on the matter. He couldn't figure out the chaos that was messing with his head regarding Emma, and he didn't see how this young buck's input on the subject would be any better. Besides, talking about Emma with one of the Double H hands seemed disrespectful to her, even if she wasn't aware of it, and he didn't want to do it.

This was not the conversation he had planned with Billy, but he might be able to use it to his advantage.

"You got yourself a girl, Billy?" asked Wes.

Billy's ears turned red and a flush crept up his neck.

"Naw. Maybe when I got more than two coins to rub together." Obviously not opposed to the idea, Billy was just realistic about his current prospects.

"Ahh, you're a bit young yet, anyway. Still, plenty of time," responded Wes.

Billy instantly sat straighter in the saddle. "I ain't that young, Wes. I'm nineteen, a man. I just looks young, that's all."

It was the perfect chance to ask Billy more questions.

"You could still be working a family farm at nineteen," Wes declared. "You have family out this way?"

Immediately Billy's shoulders slumped. "Not really. Least none I'd bother claiming."

It was said with contempt and Wes pricked up his ears thinking he might finally be getting somewhere. He'd been waiting for the opportunity to ask Billy about his family without the questions coming from nowhere.

"Yeah, you can't choose your family." Wes hoped commiseration would keep the boy talking.

"Sure wish I could have. You got family you ain't proud of too? You talk pretty nice for a cowpoke, but maybe you wasn't always doing this sorta work. 'Course, it don't matter much. Everybody has their own story; how you talk don't mean you're a good or bad person. It just is what it is."

Wes could see why it was that everyone got along with Billy; he obviously hadn't had it easy growing up, but he still seemed to be trying. Trying is what made the measure of a man, nothing else. It was like saying a rich man worked harder than a poor one. Wes had met plenty of men with deep pockets who hadn't known a day of work in their lives, and it showed. He'd also known poor men, good, honorable men, who worked day and night to provide for their families, never giving up when the times were hard. Those were the men who held his respect most.

"I'll agree with you there," Wes said, nodding. "And you're right; I do talk pretty." He gave Billy a wink.

Billy snorted, then spoke. "Though, if I was pickin', I would have kept my ma. Never had no brothers or sisters, but she was a real lady; sounded like you."

Wes barked out a laugh. "You trying to tell me that I sound like a lady, Billy McCarty?"

His eyes widened, realizing the insult in what he'd said, making Wes laugh even more. "No, no! That's not what I meant. I only meant that she had lots of learning, but my pa wouldn't put up with her teaching me all that. Said she was too uppity as it was, she wasn't goin' to make his son all woman-soft too." Billy shrugged.

"Your mother's passed then?" asked Wes.

Billy nodded. "Yes, sir."

Wes could see the pain that clouded Billy's eyes, and he could feel it too. He knew that kind of hurt all too well.

"It wasn't long after her last breath that I high-tailed it outta that house. My pa was meaner than a rattlesnake, just like the rest of his people." Billy blew out a breath that rattled his lips. "Buncha outlaws and ruffians. Not a decent one in the bunch. I'm ashamed to share their name some days."

This was exactly the conversation that Wes had been wanting to have with Billy since the moment he'd stepped onto the Double H. But where he ought to be happy to be getting around to speaking about Billy's family, the reality of what the young fella had been living through dampened his enthusiasm.

"You have nothing to be ashamed of. Your surname doesn't decide the man you become."

Billy's mouth held a grim twist with his response. "I know Ma was ashamed. She said she regretted her 'I dos' but she never regretted me."

"She sounds like she was a real good ma, Billy," assured Wes.

"She was." Billy wiped his brow and then his cheek with the back of his hand. "But what's done is done. I'm waiting for the time when I can hold my head high when folks hear my name."

Wes felt bad for pressing, but while he felt for Billy, he still had a job to do, and if he stopped asking questions each time he got to sympathizing with someone, he'd be one sorry marshal indeed.

"You ever talk to your pa?"

"Naw, he finally drowned himself at the bottom of a bottle. Can't say's I'm sorry. Truth is, makes it easier," confessed Billy. "I'm my own man now. Thanks to the Harts, I got a chance to start my life my own way."

"Glad to hear it, Billy." And Wes meant it. Young McCarty deserved a fresh start.

A sheepish grin spread across Billy's face. "I expect that was chattier than you was looking for. Probably thought you'd get a nice quiet ride back. Ma always said that I was a real talker from the time I was a little squirt. She said she never had to guess what I was thinking. I was already sayin' it."

Billy didn't know how wrong he was. Wes had gotten more information from the innocent Billy than Wes could have ever expected. It was almost certain that Billy McCarty was related to Creed and Felix, and if the way he'd described his father and age were any indicator, Wes was guessing they were his uncles.

There was no way that Billy was involved, and he was probably a dead end for a lead in tracking Creed and Felix. Perhaps he should have been more disappointed, but he was more relieved than anything. He was glad Billy had found a way to move on from his family's past and hadn't been sucked in. It would have been easy to fall prey to such a fate, but Billy had pulled himself up and out of the muck.

They rode on in relative silence, and when they got within sight of the main house of the Double H, Wes found himself looking for signs of Emma. He was going to have to take his leave of the Double H soon and knew that even if it caused him pain afterward, a few more stolen moments of Emma's time would be worth the aftermath. It would be something he could look back on in the years to come. Not so much the girl that got away, but the girl that could never be his.

He could smell the meal that Stink was fixing as they rode into the yard, and his stomach rumbled in response. He hadn't asked where the cook had gotten his moniker. When he'd first heard it applied he hadn't held much hope for the quality of the bunkhouse fare, but he had been pleasantly surprised. It shouldn't have been a shock, as good food was almost as important as wages with wranglers and ranch hands. If a man's belly wasn't happy and full, it was hard to keep him around. The Harts apparently had that figured out too.

He was turning Bass out into the corral after giving him a long brush-down, when he heard Early calling him. Gideon was waiting to speak to him at the main house, and Wes was to head there once he finished up.

After a few extra ear scratches for Bass, Wes sent the horse off to enjoy a good roll in the dust and dirt, then made his way to find out what Gideon wanted to talk about.

～

PRACTICING LETTERS WITH TILLY, Emma heard Gideon tell Early to send Wes in when he and Billy got back from Nora's. She spent the next several hours with one eye in the direction of her best friend's place, waiting for the men to appear in the distance. Wanting to be privy to the matter under discussion, Emma didn't want to miss the moment that Wes re-entered the yard.

She had spent the time after leaving Nora's place rehashing each nuance and look that had passed between her and Wes, and was still distracted as she traced the letters of the alphabet with Tilly. Thankfully, Tilly's education at this point didn't require an enormous amount of concentration on Emma's part. If it had, poor Tilly would have definitely received the short end of the stick today.

"Are you woolgathering, Auntie Emma?" asked Tilly.

Shaken from her reverie by her niece's question, Emma looked down to see that she had been drawing hearts instead of letters while Tilly had completed the entire alphabet.

She quickly took the cloth and wiped her slate clean. Thank goodness it had only been Tilly to witness the embarrassing evidence of her daydreaming.

"I was, but I see you have done a fine job at focusing. Your letters look wonderful, Tilly."

The little girl beamed under the praise, her hazel eyes staring up into Emma's. Tilly looked so much like her mother, Cordelia. Emma wondered if, some day, she might have a daughter who would share her features. The idea of having a child of her very own was a wish she had held in her heart for as long as she could remember. She never saw her other wishes, for adventure and excitement, as a barrier to motherhood.

Her own mother was a perfect example. Logan and Elizabeth Hart had picked up and left everything they knew, to start a fresh life together in the West. They hadn't known what the future held, and the arrival of their firstborn hadn't stopped their adventures. Neither had the following five children. Her mother and father had been taken far too early, but they had packed a lot of living and loving in the years they'd had.

Emma heard the main door open, and when she rose to see if Wes was finally arriving, she was stopped by Teresa.

"My girls! Come help me in the kitchen. Your young hands are required."

Neither Tilly or Emma could refuse their beloved Teresa, nor would they want to. She had taken on the role of mother and grandmother to both of them and, while she ruled the house with love, it was always with a hint of iron. Even her brothers dared not cross Teresa.

Sometimes Emma was certain Teresa could read her mind, even from another room, and intentionally thwarted her plans to prevent Emma from misbehaving. This felt a little like one of those times.

Clearing the table of their writing supplies, Emma and Tilly followed Teresa to the kitchen, like little ducklings after their mother. Emma's pride was soothed only by the memory of the many times she had watched her brothers follow along behind Teresa just as she and Tilly were doing now. She could almost hear her mother's laughter from the heavens.

After what seemed like an eternity, Emma snuck off to the library, hoping that Wes would still be inside.

Running lightly down to the hall towards the office, she could see the door was halfway open, and Emma thought she had missed her opportunity. She was about to let out an exasperated sigh when she heard Wes's voice.

He was still there!

It was difficult to be sure, but it sounded like Gideon, Luke, Ben, and Rhett were also within. With the door open, hiding her presence would be impossible; she would have to walk past slowly and hope that she would go unnoticed, while picking up whatever snippets of conversation she could. She walked past once, and when that seemed to go unnoticed, Emma dared to walk past again.

That was a mistake.

"Are you eavesdropping again, Emma?"

It was Rhett who put her on the spot. Perhaps if she had looked straight ahead as she passed, she wouldn't have caught his eye. Her hopes of glimpsing Wes had been her downfall.

Long ago, Emma had learned that with brothers, the best defense was a good offense.

"I beg your pardon, Rhett? I have no idea why you would make such an accusation. I am on my way to the kitchen and was merely walking slowly."

The heavy door groaned as it was pulled completely open, revealing Emma to the five men inside. When her eyes met Wes's, she could see the question and amusement on his face.

"Did you say, 'walking slowly'?" asked Gideon.

"Yes. That's exactly what I said. Aren't you constantly reminding me that I'm not running a race? Even following your advice, I meet with disapproval."

She was impressed by her own audacity and had to fight to hold her air of offended dignity in place. Gideon's eyebrow almost hit the ceiling as it arched upward in question.

Ben laughed out loud. "That's a fresh one, Emma!" He turned to his brothers. "She's not eavesdropping, brothers, she's practicing walking like a lady. Ha!" He paused, mock-thoughtfully. "Although, to be fair, Father did used to say she'd make a jackrabbit look slow."

"Is there something you needed, Emma?" Gideon was growing tired of the entire scene.

It was obvious that she had failed in her attempts to glean more information about Wes's presence at the Double H. Instead of holding her ground and straight-out asking what it was she wanted to know, she decided to leave while she still maintained at least some dignity.

"Other than a little respect, which obviously can't be found here, no." Spinning on her heel, she walked slowly and uprightly away, ignoring Luke's shout wishing her luck as she went.

Emma made it through the hallway and went directly to her bedroom. Shutting the door firmly, although quietly, she flopped down on her bed. What was it about having brothers that made her act the child? She had barely prevented herself from stomping off and thereby humiliating herself in front of Wes. Emma wasn't sure if it was the chicken or the egg: which came first? Did she remain a child in her brothers' eyes because she acted that way, or was it impossible for them to consider her a grown woman, so she met their low expectations?

Either way, it was her responsibility to change their minds or her ways. She needed to prove she was as capable as they were. She just needed an opportunity.

9

Wes awoke with a start.

He looked around as he wiped the cold sweat from his brow and neck, then tried to focus his eyes. It took a moment to remember where he was, the snores and sounds of the other ranch hands at sleep helping him to center himself.

The Dream.

It had been a long time since it had last come to him. Wes hadn't figured that it had left for good, but he enjoyed respite during the interval.

It always started the same way: his father pushing him under his bed and telling him to stay down, not to come out until he called for him or returned. Wes listening as his mother, too, was warned to stay inside and out of sight. Then Father leaving to go speak with the men who were waiting for him by their family barn.

Young Wes watched from his hiding spot in their small home as his mother paced back and forth across their oak plank floors, and he lay on his stomach, trembling beneath the rough-hewn frame of the bed his father had made for him.

Even in his dreams, the memory was hazy, the events seen through the eyes of a young child. His mother seemed to be moving in slow motion, yet it all happened so fast. Grabbing the gun from above the stone fireplace, she had flung open the front door to their home. He heard the shot first, then watched helplessly as his mother fell to the floor, still in the doorway, never having fired a round of her own.

Him, scrambling from beneath the bed to her side, her bright blue eyes, so like his own, closed, her chest no longer moving.

Shouting outside, and more shots fired, but Wes didn't know who had been hit. It was only once his father ran back to the house, and thrust him away from his mother's body, that Wes peeked out and saw the lifeless bodies of the two men in their yard. He tried to get back to his mother but was shoved to the side as his father cradled her in his arms and screamed out in grief. Frightened, young Wes slunk back beneath the bed, pressing his little hands to his ears, trying to stop the wailing cries of his father from reaching him.

A shudder went through him, and adult Wes pulled his woolen blanket closer to his chin, unsure of whether it was the cool night air or the memory that left him feeling chilled.

He wondered, only for a moment, what had resurrected the dream. The truth was, he knew exactly what caused it, and what it meant.

In his days undercover at the Double H, despite his best efforts, he found himself seeking out Emma Hart at every opportunity. He spent too much time watching her while he was supposed to be working, and he had the sore thumbs to prove it. The desire to see her, to speak to her, was so strong that it couldn't be thwarted. Emma's very existence distracted him to no end, and it seemed he was powerless to control what he was feeling for her.

His attempts to keep his guard up had been a complete failure. Instead, he was allowing her to break down his carefully constructed walls by simply being...Emma. Bright, funny, beautiful Emma.

Wes closed his eyes, and the vision of her heart-shaped face and those deep brown eyes floated across to him. She was lovely, but there was more to what he felt than an attraction to her face and form. A pretty girl could be found in any town or city. There was something far greater than beauty that pulled him to Emma Hart.

The rhythm of life at the Double H held a lot of appeal. He knew so little of ranching, and while the work they had assigned him wasn't always easy, it provided a beginning and end each day, and Wes liked that. The camaraderie of the men made the work more enjoyable too. There were good people at the Double H.

But it was Emma who kept pulling him in. He watched as she attended to her chores and as she spent time with Tilly out in the yard. Wes wished he could see what they did in the big house as well.

He felt a pang of loss for something he never thought he'd have, and never even realized he wanted. A family. A wife and children of his own, whose laughter would fill his days and be a balm to his soul. Wes had started to believe that maybe he'd been wrong, and the lesson his father had driven home over the years had been misguided. That maybe he could share his life with a good woman. With Emma. But then reality kicked in, and The Dream had come back to remind him.

Wes let out a long, slow breath.

Thoughts of Emma had taken over his days and nights. There was no escaping her, and a part of Wes wondered if he even wanted to. She was all-consuming; he craved her. No, his sweet tooth craved sugar, and normally a candy would be enough to satisfy, but this wanting, this longing was something else altogether.

Wes wanted Emma, but it wasn't in the carnal way that left a man feeling spent and empty. He wanted Emma to be his, to hold her when she needed him, to have her at his side as they grew old together. Wes wanted Emma as his wife, to hear people call out 'Mrs. Hayes' when they passed, and to be himself, the proud father of their children.

That was what he wanted, and that was what he could never have. So instead, he played a fool's game, pretending in his mind that it could even be possible.

His heart and mind fought a battle each day, which left him friendly one day, then closed-off the next. He had also promised her brothers, when they had generously allowed him to do his work on their land, that he would stay away from Emma, and he'd wanted to respect that. Still, Wes wondered, if they knew his intentions to be honorable, would they allow him to ask for her hand?

It had all gone sideways.

Wes rested his forearm across his brow, covering his eyes. How had he thought this was going to end? What did he think would happen? Was he going to give up the life he knew, the only job he had ever done, to become a rancher? He'd only been a child when they lived on the family farm. His father had moved them to town after his mother's death. What did he know about ranching? It wasn't just riding horses and building fences; there was so much more to it than that. The past week had proven that in spades.

And if he stayed a marshal?

He couldn't be a lawman and be married. Not to any woman, and certainly not to Emma. She was impetuous, and she'd been cradled in the safe cocoon of the Double H Ranch and the security of having five brothers.

Emma had never learned to respect the dangers of the outside world, and it led her to tread fearlessly through the world in her innocence. She was blessed to have lived so freely; Wes didn't begrudge her that luxury. He wanted that for all people, from all walks of life. It was part of the reason he'd chosen the profession he had. What he didn't want was his world of bad men and bandits to collide with hers.

While her bold nature and zest for life were part of what drew Emma to him, they were also the things that frightened him the most. His mother had never been one to listen to anyone and, in the moment where it mattered most, she had not heeded the advice that would have saved her life. Wes couldn't bear the thought of something happening to Emma because of the life he had chosen.

No, he was doing the right thing by leaving the Double H, and Emma. Gideon had asked for the interview with him yesterday to learn of his progress with Billy McCarty. When Wes shared his conversation with Billy with the Hart brothers, they all agreed that a good effort had been made, but that it was time for the ruse to be over and for Wes to move on. He retrieved his badge and papers, no longer needing them hidden.

The reality was, he probably hadn't needed to go through all the subterfuge to get what he wanted from Billy. Luke had been right—Wes should have just asked Billy straight out; the kid was a talker anyway. Deep down, Wes knew that he had gone through all these machinations to be near Emma. It had been a mistake. All he'd done was let the McCartys get further away and drive himself mad with longing for a woman he couldn't have. He wasn't used to failing at his job, but in the week he'd spent at the Double H, he had won nothing and lost far more.

It had been near the end of their meeting that Emma had been caught eavesdropping at the door of the library. Despite the heavy weight in his heart, Wes found himself smiling in the dark, at the antics of Miss Emma Hart when she'd been caught.

In a glorious show of innocence that would have made any theater performer proud, she tried to turn the tables. Like a child with crumbs on her face claiming she hadn't eaten the last cookie. Who did she think she was fooling?

Although thankful she was not, Wes thought that if Emma were a man, he would have loved to have played a hand or two of cards against her. He would have easily emptied her pockets by the end of the night.

The strange thing was, the fact that she was a terrible liar made her even more endearing. One would think that her attempts to dupe them would be irritating or, at the very least, off-putting, but instead it had had the opposite effect. It made her more captivating. She had to cope somehow. Wes had no idea how he would have survived having five older brothers. One had to use all the tactics at one's disposal. Unfortunately for Emma, her brothers could see right through her.

Wes sighed. This was all a mess of his own making. The only person he had to blame was himself, and the only person he should be feeling sorry for should be Emma. He'd allowed this charade to go on too long, and to go too far. Emma didn't deserve to be put into this kind of situation. It wasn't fair.

Letting her think that there was even a chance had been cruel, and Wes would regret what he had done for the rest of his days. It had never been his intention; in fact, he had tried to remain indifferent. But Emma, with her engaging smile and spirited personality, had been too great a temptation to resist.

His efforts to ignore her had been an utter disaster. There were moments he was amazed that Emma was still on speaking terms with him, after his displays of unpredictable moods and volatility. She was too forgiving, too kind, and too good for him.

He had to leave. The McCartys weren't going to turn themselves in, and he still had a job he was contracted to do, which he had to see through. It was strange, how his lifelong desire for justice didn't rouse him in the same way it once had. He wouldn't leave without saying goodbye: that would have been an unforgiveable insult. The truth was that he wanted to see her, to speak with her one last time. After that he would ride out and move on, leaving his heart behind.

10

Emma rested her chin on her folded hands while she leaned against the fresh section of corral fence that Wes and Billy had recently fixed.

The sun hadn't been up long, but Tilly had been eager to practice trotting with her pony, Domino. Thankfully the black and white spotted pony was a good-natured creature, as Tilly had the personality of a Hart and preferred to do things her way. With most men and beasts, they were often most reasonable just after a night of rest. The same could be said for Domino's current rider.

Her eyes drifted to Early, who was standing inside the corral, ready to offer assistance if needed. Emma had been too young to remember, but it had probably been the same scene playing out when she was Tilly's age.

Like Tilly, Emma had grown up following the kind wrangler as though she were his shadow. He never complained, although many times, she knew she had tested his patience.

Early's ebony skin was like leather, and the wrinkles that outlined his eyes had grown deeper over the years. Hair more grey than black these days, Early's years were starting to show but that wide smile was still hard to resist, and if he shared it with you, there was little chance you weren't returning it. He had a heart-shaped birthmark just below his ear, and Emma could remember as a child being jealous that she didn't have one too. To her, as well as her brothers, Early was as much a part of the Double H as the very land she stood on.

He'd been Isiah Wells when he had left the South after the end of the war. After hearing of the death of his wife and two young daughters. He had never even had the chance to say goodbye, as they had been taken, and sent to another plantation before their deaths. Nursing a broken heart, he was seeking a place to live out the second half of his life, a freed man, and soon Isiah joined up with a group of cowpokes and learned to be wrangler.

It was at the tail-end of a combined cattle drive when Isiah Wells met Emma's father. The two men had hit it off immediately and become fast friends. Appreciating the man's way with both man and beast, Logan Hart had offered him a place at the Double H. Isiah accepted the offer. He'd gotten the nickname Early when he showed up to start work a day earlier than her father had expected. Gideon had only been knee-high to a grasshopper at that time, and when he heard his father say, "You're Early," Gideon assumed it was the man's name, and the moniker stuck. 'Early' had been an integral part of the ranch ever since.

Emma smiled as she listened to Early teach Tilly horsemanship through his tall tales. He had done the same with her, and she had heard this particular one before. The man was a natural-born storyteller, and Emma still found herself enjoying the yarn, although she was certain when he'd last told it that the cows' names were Daisy and Cupcake. This time around he'd switched them to Buttercup and Nutmeg.

"She's doing well," observed Emma, once Tilly resumed her riding, keeping her voice low.

"Didn't expect different," replied Early. "You Harts were born in the saddle."

"Cordelia didn't like riding," Emma remembered. "In fact, as I recall, she hated it."

Early's jaw clenched, and then released, at the mention of Tilly's mother. "That little girl ain't nothing like her mother." He turned briefly to Emma. "Sorry, Emma; I shouldn't let my tongue get away from me like that."

The hard words were a shock, coming from Early. Emma couldn't recall him saying an unkind word about anyone. Cordelia hadn't been the easiest person to get along with, but she was still Tilly's mother and Gideon's wife. She was about to ask him what he meant when Tilly cried out, "Mr. Hayes!!"

Emma turned to see Wes walking out of the bunkhouse. How had Tilly seen him so quickly? She was supposed to be concentrating, not hollering across the yard. Wes waved back, and Emma could see his pearly white teeth from the corral. Her tongue swiped across her own. She didn't think she had teeth that sparkling, though she put full effort into maintaining them. Knowing Wes's sweet tooth, she pictured him up half the night, scrubbing his teeth to perfection.

A quiet chuckle from Early made Emma turn back to the corral. "What?"

"Don't worry. You look right pretty, Emma," the old man said, smiling.

Emma shot Early a look. "What are you talking about?"

"Can't see why else you suddenly pat down that hair, smooth your skirts and stand up straight, all at the sound of one man's name." Early shrugged. "My mistake, guess I'm just getting old."

Early could see right through her, and there was no point in denying it. The truth was she hadn't realized she had done any of those things. Once again, Wes was catching her looking less than her best. Her visit to Nora's had been the only time she'd had on clean clothes and combed hair. All the other moments they had run into each other at the ranch had been poorly timed, grooming wise.

Sighing, Emma waved to Wes, who returned the gesture with a nod. He was turning back to the bunkhouse when Tilly called out again.

"Come watch what I can do, Mr. Hayes! Come watch me and Domino!"

Wes hesitated, looking behind him, then started to walk over. Emma laughed inwardly. Tilly seemed to have the marshal wrapped around her finger, like everyone else who set foot on the Double H.

She tried not to blatantly stare as he sauntered over to the corral. His long, strong legs made short work of the distance, and his cotton shirt was snug in all the right places. It was still early in the day, but Emma was already starting to feel heated.

"Mornin', Wes," Early said, nodding.

"Morning." He glanced over at Emma. "Miss Emma."

Emma could see the barely suppressed smirk on Early's face and realized that the old ranch hand must like Wes very much; otherwise, he wouldn't be entertained by her antics at Wes's presence.

"Think I'll go give Tilly a hand. I'm betting she'll want to show you a few tricks."

Early left the two of them alone.

"Domino. It's a fitting name," said Wes.

"It was almost Mr. Hoofington, but when she discovered it was a mare Tilly went with Domino instead."

Why had she just said that? What a crude story to have told. Emma wondered if Wes thought her to be beyond censure at this point.

Wes chuckled, his twinkling blue eyes a stark contrast to his sun-touched face. Emma was amazed at how a man could be so rugged and still remain handsome. Yet, there was no denying it as Wes stood before her, fitting the description perfectly.

She wasn't sure which Wes would be at her side while they watched Tilly and Early. Would it be the man from the mercantile and Nora's, or the one who looked like she was giving him toothache because she merely existed? So far, he seemed pleased to be in her company.

Emma enjoyed the comfortable silence that fell between them as they applauded Tilly on her newly acquired skills. The little girl was especially excited to show them how she could get Domino to jump over a log. Of course, the pony's legs never really left the ground, unless stepping over the log one leg at a time counted. Wes was a true gentleman and cheered on Tilly's mighty jump.

His consideration of Tilly's pride and feelings was another check in his favor. In fact, there was no box the man hadn't ticked off for her. It was just his nearness to her now that made her feel warm and excited. When Wes was close to her, her heart beat faster and she wanted him to put his arms around her. It was as though all her nerves were firing at once, and she didn't know what to do.

Was this love? Was this what books and plays meant when they spoke of passion and love? It wasn't the heart-pounding excitement of adventure; she had experienced that before. This was something different, something new, and it filled her completely. Emma wanted more of this feeling, the one that made her pulse race and a heat radiate throughout her chest. A vision of a man cradling a dark-haired, blue-eyed baby in his arms flashed into her mind, and when Emma saw that the man was Wes, she knew.

She loved him.

Emma didn't want to play games with him anymore. She wanted Wes to tell her who he really was, to share his story with her. The secret that both held from each other needed to be spoken aloud. She could keep his confidence; he didn't have to doubt her. Emma could be impatient and impulsive at times, but she was not untrustworthy. She wanted Wes to understand that.

"I know you're a deputy marshal."

She'd said it, and there was no taking it back. Holding in a breath, watching Tilly so she wouldn't need to look at him, Emma waited for him to respond.

He let out a long sigh. "I'm sorry for my need to be deceptive, Miss Emma."

Emma hadn't expected an apology. His response surprised her. "You can call me Emma, if you like ...Wes."

She heard him suck back in the breath he'd just exhaled. "Emma. How did you find out?"

He said it with such reverence that, for the first time in her life, her name sounded beautiful.

"I overheard my brothers."

"So, you were eavesdropping last night. And here I thought your brothers were unfairly maligning you," he said, smiling.

"No. Well, yes. I actually overheard it by accident, the day you rode into the Double H," said Emma.

"Overheard?" His question was a teasing one.

With an embarrassed laugh, Emma replied. "Inadvertently yes. I unsuccessfully tried to eavesdrop on the rest of the conversation, but it was to no avail. You closed the door."

"And last night ... asked Wes.

"I thought I told you all, I was merely walking slowly," said Emma, doing her best to sound dignified.

"You're an awful liar," laughed Wes.

Emma smiled. She was relieved to finally have the truth out in the open. Already, Wes seemed more relaxed. Whether it was due to their open conversation or to something else was yet to be seen.

"Tell me something, Wes. If I were a man, would you have told me who you were?"

"I only told Gideon and Luke. It was their decision to tell Ben and Rhett," replied Wes.

"Sometimes I wish I was a man," sighed Emma.

"I'm glad you're not ..." His voice trailed off. It was obvious that Wes hadn't intended to speak those words out loud. Emma thought the color that suddenly found his cheeks was quite endearing.

"Did you see that?" Tilly shouted with excitement. "I'm so good! I can do anything. Right, Early? Maybe we can try bulldogging this afternoon!"

"Oh, heavens, Gideon's going to kill me," murmured Emma. "Sometimes that child has me worried it will be Tilly you're chasing after one of these days."

"How'd you guess that Tilly's actually the reason I'm here?" His fake surprise caused Emma to let out a most unladylike burst of laughter.

"Don't tease. That thought keeps me up some nights." Emma waited a moment, and then spoke again. "Why *are* you here at the Double H...Wes?"

Wes looked at her as though trying to decide if she could be trusted. He must have determined she was, because he shared the entire story. He left out the details of what Creed and Felix McCarty had done, but explained why it was that he needed to be undercover at the Double H.

Glad that Billy McCarty wasn't a part of the outlaws' criminal activities, Emma still felt awful for sweet Billy and what he must have lived through, being connected to such a family. She told herself to give extra thanks tonight for having the great fortune of being born into such a loving home.

Emma was still interested in Wes's work as a marshal and asked him to share some stories. He told her a few tales, but Emma could tell he was tempering what he told her. He probably thought if he revealed too much, she would dissolve into tears and go running to her brothers. She hoped there would come a time when Wes would come to see she was made of tougher stuff than that.

"The truth is, Emma, that often, men give themselves up after a long chase. For some, they've been running so long, that being caught and getting guaranteed meals and a roof over their heads starts to sound appealing," shared Wes.

"The ones not bound for the gallows, anyway," replied Emma.

Shocked, Wes nearly choked on her words. "Yes, except those ones."

He shook his head at her audacious statement. Emma wondered if he was more shocked or impressed. The look in his eyes seemed to indicate he was a bit of both.

"You sure you want to hear all the things I do as a marshal, Emma? I can't imagine that these are the types of stories that you ladies might hear at a quilting bee."

"You seem to be very sure of what conversation takes place when women gather, Wes. I think you might be surprised," declared Emma. "Although, when men walk through the door, we do go back to sipping our tea daintily and only talking about the hard work of men."

"Fair enough. The truth is I've never attended a quilting bee," acknowledged Wes. "I'll defer to your expertise on such matters."

"My 'expertise' there is rather limited. That's why I am so interested in your work. There is so much in the world to see, to do," sighed Emma. "You are so lucky."

"Lucky?" said Wes, as he rubbed the back of his neck, the soft waves of black between his fingers. "Don't know if I'd ever describe it that way. Fulfilling, maybe. I've never known anything else, so I wouldn't know any different."

"I'm not saying that I want to be a lawman—"

"That's why it's lawman, not law lady."

Emma threw Wes a withering look, then continued. "I have never been away from Autumn Springs or the Double H. Not really. I want to see … more."

"What exactly do you think 'more' is, Emma?" asked Wes. "Most people are searching for exactly what you've got right here."

She knew that was true, and she was grateful, but that didn't stop her from yearning. "I'd like to see an ocean, or a city so big that you couldn't walk it in one day. I want to eat something I have never even seen before, never even heard of." Emma paused, thinking for a moment, then continued. "And I'd like to see a play."

"A play." He seemed surprised.

"Yes. A play in a real theater, with a real orchestra." Emma had wondered what that would be like her entire life. Cordelia had talked about such things, how much better the city was, and it had made Emma long to see it for herself. "Autumn Springs is a wonderful little town and it's growing fast. But who knows when and if it will ever have something like that? At least during my lifetime."

"That's a lot to want," remarked Wes.

"Is it?" sighed Emma. "Perhaps, but I want it anyway."

She looked over to Wes. "What about you? Don't you want things?"

"I do, but I also have accepted what is and is not possible. Recognizing the difference has made my life much easier, and certainly more bearable."

"Has it? I don't think I would like a life that is merely ... bearable."

"Nor should you accept one, Emma Hart."

He said it softly, and their eyes met. A shiver rippled across her skin, and Emma saw a longing that matched her own reflected in his eyes. She reached out a hand, but Wes stepped back. Embarrassed, Emma folded her hands in front of her.

"I'm sorry, Emma," whispered Wes.

She shook her head. "The apology is mine, Mr. Hayes. I thought that there was something between us. I was mistaken."

"There was—there is," Wes growled. "It's my fault. I've gone about this all wrong. I never should have led you to believe..." He let the words trail off.

"Believe what?" Emma had turned away from Tilly and Early and was now standing facing him directly.

He shook his head. "That I—that we—I'm not the right man for you, Emma. I can't be. Not with my work, not with who I am."

"A marshal? That's your concern?"

"Yes, that's part of it. A woman shouldn't be subjected to the inherent dangers that come with the life I lead," said Wes. "It's not safe."

"Not safe?" Her eyes narrowed. "Correct me if I'm wrong, but you're saying that you *do* feel something in your heart for me, but because you're a *deputy US marshal*, you can't pursue it? That there's a clause in your marshal contract that says you aren't allowed to love, because of the danger? That women are too fragile, not only to be lawmen, but to even be subjected to the presence of one."

Wes glanced back to the corral, then back to her, his voice low. "Don't go and twist my words, Emma. I'm trying to tell you that I want you to be safe."

"Safe? You think you're the only one that can look after themselves and shoot a gun? I may be a woman, but I am still a Hart, and if given the chance, I'm sure I could take down Creed and Felix McCarty as easily as you. If I were a man, I'd bet you just that!"

Arms crossed, she continued. "I'm a dead shot, *Marshal*. Just because I don't walk around with a gun belt swinging from my hips doesn't mean I can't take care of myself."

Emma wasn't done. "I've been barred from competing in Autumn Springs Annual Turkey Shoot. And don't tell me it's because I'm a girl. They only put that rule in place after I kept winning."

Wes took off his hat and ran his fingers through his hair before putting it back on. He opened his mouth to speak, and then shut it again. He gripped the top of the corral post he'd recently put in, and Emma saw his knuckles grow white as he tried to master himself.

"This. This is what I mean. Now, I'm not saying that you should be staying inside to spend your days on embroidery or that sort of thing, but I am saying that marshal business, *federal* business, is not your concern."

Emma wished she could embroider her thoughts

regarding Wes's high and mighty attitude across his forehead.

"The last thing I need to be worried about is you and your safety when I have a job to do. You asked if it was only because of my job that I wasn't the right man for you? Well, it's also the fact that you're standing here, all but threatening to go off and put yourself in danger without even thinking twice. You're good with a saucy line, I'll give you that, but you have no idea what it's like when real trouble comes calling."

Emma felt her hackles rise. Not ten minutes ago, she had realized she was in love, and now she realized that the man she had fallen head over heels for was the same sort of stubborn, pig-headed man her brothers were. And while her heart had made its decision, her head and her mouth did not agree.

"You are entitled to your opinion, as I am entitled to mine," stated Emma, coldly.

"It's not an opinion, Emma, it's a fact," said Wes through thin lips.

"In case you haven't noticed, I'm not some helpless debutante."

"Be a whole lot easier to handle," retorted Wes.

Emma's mouth opened, then she snapped it shut, pinching her lips together. She could feel her face and neck flushing with heat.

She was done fighting. There was no talking to the man, and she knew that he wasn't listening anyway. They both needed to step away from each other.

Drawing herself up to her full height, she squared her shoulders. "I'm sure you have some work to do, and I think it's best you go do that. You wouldn't want people to think you were any more than an employee of the Double H."

"I'll be leaving today, anyway. I told Gideon I'd ride out with him and some of the boys to the east boundary to see if I can help with the problem of some missing cattle. Fence was down out there. But after that, I'm gone. Since Billy hasn't been the lead I needed, there's no reason for me to stay here."

His words struck her like a bucket of ice, and she went completely still. For a moment, the lump in her throat left her speechless to reply.

"No reason at all?" Emma asked quietly, her anger cooled by the realization that Wes would soon be gone.

He looked pained. He squeezed his eyebrows together, and she saw him take a steeling breath before he responded. "I have to go, Emma."

Wes was leaving the Double H and after today, she would never see him again. She felt a knot in her belly and quickly regretted the harsh words they'd just exchanged.

Perhaps it was for the best. He didn't see a path forward for the two of them, and Emma didn't want to be with a man who she had to convince to love her.

Unrequited love. It seemed that Deputy US Marshal Weston Hayes was going to provide her with a new experience after all.

"I wish you well … Wes."

"Emma." Wes tipped his hat, and then he walked back to the bunkhouse.

She didn't watch him go; she couldn't. Instead, she bit the inside of her lip to keep the tears from flowing.

Early glanced over, a questioning look on his face, while Tilly yelled out her goodbye to Wes, not realizing the finality of the words.

"Keep going!" Emma called out to Tilly, but maybe she meant the instruction for herself.

She had no choice. Breaking heart or not, she had obligations and chores to attend to. Emma would take Nora's advice. Stay busy and distracted and push the pain from your heart.

Keep going.

11

With Tilly napping after an energetic morning with Early outside, Emma had time on her hands. Too much time, to think about the departure of Marshal Weston Hayes from the Double H. The peas she was shelling, out on the porch, were taking the brunt of her frustration. Only half were fit to serve after her manhandling of them. If she kept this up, there wouldn't be enough for dinner. She wished she could speak to Nora right now.

She should have worn an apron. Wiping her green fingers on the trousers she wore, Emma couldn't help but shake her head and smile ruefully. She was a mess. Two weeks ago, she would not have cared in the least, but now she was wondering if her uncanny timing at making a mess of herself another reason that Wes hadn't even tried to find a solution that could allow them to be together.

If it was money that he worried about, he didn't need to. She owned the land of the Double H as much as any of her brothers. She and Wes could carve out their own place, together.

Emma sighed. The foolish pride of men would probably have Wes thinking that was the worst idea possible, not wanting to be living off his wife's money.

Wife. Who was Emma trying to fool? Despite their obvious attraction to one another, she hadn't even been able to inspire Wes to try and court her, let alone marry. *Wife* had never even been on the table. He was certain that she wasn't even capable of looking after herself, that she had spent her days being cossetted, to the point where she would swoon at the first sign of trouble. It wasn't his profession that worried him, it was her.

Emma wished she could prove somehow to Wes that he didn't need to worry, that she could be a help, not a hindrance. But that was impossible to do when the man had insisted on leaving and was never coming back.

She was throwing another handful of shells in the scrap bowl she was saving for the hogs, when she saw Billy McCarty saddling up his mount at the back of the bunkhouse. He kept swivelling his head about, as though checking to see that no one was watching. He caught her eye and nodded in the distance. Apparently he didn't consider her a concern.

Emma stopped shelling. Whatever Billy was up to, he had her full attention.

Wes had said he didn't think Billy was involved in his family's trouble, but every one of her senses told her that something wasn't right with the scene taking place before her. With everyone out working, most of them already deep in the east pasture, Emma was the only witness to Billy's strange behavior.

What should she do? Most likely it was nothing; just her imagination running away on her again. She could almost hear her brothers' laughter, supposing she tried to tell them of her suspicions. But what if it was related to Creed and Felix McCarty? What if this was the opportunity that Wes had been waiting for, and his determination to get away from her made him miss his chance to catch the McCartys?

It didn't take her long to decide. When Tilly got up, she would seek out Teresa, hoping for a snack to fill her belly after her sleep. So, Emma had some time to go after Billy.

She didn't need to make herself known. She would stay out of sight and simply see where he was headed. She wasn't foolish enough to try and bring the McCartys in herself, although a small part of her did briefly consider it. She allowed herself a quick laugh at the look that Wes would be wearing if she did. No, she was going to be careful, but helpful, proving to Wes that his concerns about her were unwarranted, and that she actually was a real boon to a lawman.

As soon as Billy rode off southward, Emma ran to the stable and took her horse from its stall. Once she had Neptune saddled up, she followed after Billy, making sure to keep him in her sights, while trying to stay out of his.

Although it felt like she'd been riding for hours, the sun's place in the sky told her it hadn't been long. Emma wished she'd thought to bring along some water, as the heat was starting to take its toll. Thankful she had remembered to throw on a wide-brimmed hat, Emma continued to follow her quarry.

Billy was headed towards the small gorge that marked the boundary between the southern edge of the territory owned by the Double H, and Lafferty land. Emma started to wonder if Billy was doing a bit of dirty side business with the Laffertys before she remembered that the missing cattle had been over by the eastern border, and that was too far from the Laffertys. Emma shook her head at her suspicious mind. The Laffertys were good people, and here she was lumping them in with outlaws.

But Billy was definitely up to something.

The closer they got to the Echo Gorge, the more slowly Billy rode. Whatever had sent him hightailing it out from the Double H now seemed to be giving him pause. What was going on? What was he doing? It just didn't make any sense. Between the story Wes had shared and her own knowledge of Billy from around the ranch, none of this behavior seemed to fit. Wes was an experienced marshal. She doubted he would be so thoroughly duped. Why, when Billy had been quick to leave, was he now reluctant to proceed? Emma had so many questions, and not a single answer.

She watched as Billy's mount picked its way down into the canyon and then disappeared from her sight. Emma followed, but instead of descending, she found an overhang with boulders and bushes where she could stay hidden, and hopefully overhear what was taking place below. She left Neptune untied and happily munching new growth while she snuck to her vantage point. If she needed to make a break for it, she didn't need her fingers fumbling over reins.

Below, there were two men Emma had never seen before. They were both visibly dirty and haggard, like they'd been living rough for some time but in spite of the age difference, their resemblance to Billy was evident.

These men must be the outlaws Creed and Felix McCarty!

They were too far below for Emma to make out the conversation, but the sound of laughter floated up to her hiding spot. It wasn't the teasing and jovial sound she was used to from her brothers. This was nasty and cruel, and it made the hairs on the back of her neck rise.

Squeezing her eyes shut, Emma took a deep breath and evaluated her options, discovering there was only one. There was no reason for her to try and capture the McCartys. She hadn't brought a gun, she was outnumbered, and reality was kicking in. She'd found them: that was enough. Now, all she needed to do was get back to the Double H and let Wes and her brothers know what she had seen, and where.

On hands and knees, Emma slowly backed away from the rocks, trying to make as little noise as possible. The last thing she needed was to bring attention to herself. As she retreated, she felt something brush against her leg. Holding her breath, Emma peered down to see a snake slithering across the dirt, its body gliding alongside her leg.

It was a harmless garter snake. Emma knew the small, thin creature meant her no harm, but logic had nothing to do with her body's reflexive reaction to the serpent. Both Emma and Ben were terrified of snakes, ever since Ben had been bitten by a rattler years ago. Nora's father had ensured Ben kept his leg, but the incident had instilled a fear in Emma that was as intense as it was irrational.

She managed not to cry out but her sudden, panicked movements betrayed her. As she twisted away from the snake, it was enough to dislodge a few bits of gravel and stones. They tumbled and bounced down to the men, not far below. Cringing at the noise, Emma laid low, listening as they clattered to a stop. Hoping the men hadn't heard, or that if they had, they wouldn't bother to investigate the source of the rockfall, she held her breath.

Keeping one eye on the wretched reptile, Emma prayed the men would ignore the stones and carry on with their nefarious business. She cursed the garter and her foolish reaction, knowing that she was in far more danger from the McCartys if they caught her.

The snake started to slide closer to her and Emma closed her eyes, hoping that she could contain the scream she felt bubbling up inside, if only she couldn't see it. There was sudden silence from the men, and all Emma could hear was the beating of her heart, pounding in her ears. Sweat gathered beneath her neck and trickled into the dirt.

Emma didn't know how much time had passed while she remained immobile. Still hoping her silent pleas for continued concealment would be heard, she kept her eyes squeezed shut. Emma was certain the garter was waiting her out.

Nothing happened.

The snake hadn't reached her face.

Gathering her courage, Emma opened one eye to see where the serpent was. Instead, she was staring at a worn pair of dusty, black, leather boots where the snake had been.

"Well, well, well. Looky here. What do we have here?"

Emma squinted up against the sun to see the leering face of one of the McCartys.

Hair, that might be fair, hung in greasy strands below a dark brown hat. With the ruthless expression on his face and the forbidding look in his eyes, the man looked every bit the villain.

In that moment, Emma realized exactly what Wes had meant.

All her wishes for excitement and adventure fled. It was replaced by real, cold fear, and Emma recognized the enormity of the mistake she had made.

"Get up," said the man. When Emma didn't move fast enough for his liking, he grabbed her and pulled her from the ground, bruising her arm.

"Get your hands off me, you, you—"

"Careful how you finish that, girly. You ain't the one in control here."

Emma straightened to her full height and thrust her shoulders back, looking her assailant directly in the eye. "I'm not afraid of you. Do you know who I am?"

The man gave a sharp, contemptuous snort and then leaned in close to Emma's face, his sour breath enveloping them like a cloud. "I dunno who you are, but you should be scared."

"Billy! Felix!" shouted the man, who must be Creed McCarty. "Get up here! We got ourselves some company." Crossing his arms, his stance wide, he gave Emma an appraising stare. "If you're as important as you think you are, maybe Billy-boy can enlighten us."

Emma didn't bother to respond. She couldn't trust her voice to not crack or waver. She was absolutely terrified, but she didn't want Creed to know that. She didn't want to hand him any more power over her than he already had.

When Billy and Felix came into view, Emma saw Billy's eyes widen. His face turned ashen.

"Miss Emma?" Billy barely choked out her name. "What are you doing here?"

"A better question is: what are you doing here, Billy?" Emma was pleased her voice hadn't given her panic away.

"She's pretty," said Felix. It was the first thing he had said, and it came out with a kind of whistle, as he was missing one of his front teeth.

Creed gave the awful laugh again. "That she is, Brother." He looked over to Billy. "This your girl? That why she was following you out here? Worried her man might have another sweetheart?"

"She's not—"

Creed kept talking. "Ha, I always thought you was soft, Billy-boy."

Emma watched as Billy cringed at the name.

"But maybe there's a bit of your pa in you yet. He always liked them real fancy ladies. Fancy talkers, thinking they're too good for ya. Your pa never cared; he went after your ma anyway. Even after we warned him. Women like that are useless, I say. Made of weakness, and they breed weakness. Like your ma did with you. Don't know how our big brother put up with the two of you all those years. Your ma did him a favor when she up and died."

Billy's white face had turned red with rage. "How dare—"

Felix clamped a hand down hard on Billy's shoulder, holding him back from Creed.

"Whoa now, boy, don't be stupid; remember I got your girl. I'd hate to see her get hurt 'cuz you can't hold that McCarty temper in check."

Emma could see Billy's frustration and panic. It was written all over his face. She got the feeling that Billy was not a willing participant in whatever was going on.

"Don't hurt her, Uncle Creed. Please," he begged.

"Aww, now ain't that sweet?" sneered Creed.

Her fists were clenched. It was taking the utmost control for Emma not to slug Creed, but that wouldn't do any good, and she needed to keep her wits about her. She glanced over her shoulder to Neptune, who was now closer to them atop the overhang. There was no way, even in pants, that Emma could run and mount her horse before one of the McCartys caught her. There was one other possibility though.

Suddenly spinning, Emma ran for Neptune and managed to smack her poor horse hard on the rump, before

Creed grabbed hold of her arm and swung her around. Neptune didn't wait around to be hit again.

"Nice try, girly," said Creed as he tightened his grip on her arm and pulled her in close, snarling "Try something like that again, and I'll put a bullet hole right through the boy."

She shivered at the warning. Emma didn't doubt the outlaw would follow through on his threat and was grateful she wouldn't need to try again. She had accomplished what she wanted, spooking Neptune enough that the well-trained horse would head straight back to the Double H. When Neptune arrived in the yard, saddled, but without her, they would know something was wrong.

Billy shrugged off Felix and glared at Creed. "You're making a big mistake. That's Miss Emma Hart of the Double H. You should let her go."

Emma watched with satisfaction as the brothers paled at Billy's mention of her family name. She was suddenly much more appreciative of her family name. "Perhaps you've met my brothers? If not, you soon will." Her sweet tone belied the forewarning in her words.

Felix swallowed audibly. He didn't bother to hide his worry as he tugged at his brother's coat sleeve. "Creed, we don't need no extra trouble. Things is bad enough. We better let her go."

Emma could tell Creed was nervous too. He loosened the filthy scarf from around his throat and rolled his neck back and forth. To his credit, he was putting up a good front for his brother and nephew, waving away Felix's concern like it was a minor inconvenience.

"Don't you worry none, Brother. If Billy-boy here does what he's supposed to do, then by the time this little filly makes it home, we'll be long gone."

"You're despicable," Emma spat out. She had never met such awful people before and knowing that Billy had grown up under such influences was heartbreaking. How he had turned out to be such a kind, hard-working person, she'd never understand. He had obviously been pulled into a mess that wasn't of his own making. She hoped her brothers wouldn't blame him.

"I'm so...so sorry, Miss Emma," stuttered Billy. She could see the regret and guilt as clear as day on his face.

"It's not your fault. I followed you." Her assurance did little to comfort him. He shook his head, avoiding her gaze.

"Aw, well, ain't this sweet. The fancy, rich girl might be sweet on you after all, Billy," jeered Creed. Felix sniggered at Creed's mockery of their nephew. "Guess that's why you never wanted to team up with us. Your ma had you thinking you were better than the rest of us McCartys. Well, it ain't true, boy. You're just spendin' your days working to fill another man's pockets 'stead of your own."

"It's honest work for honest wages. The Harts are good people," said Billy, straightening his back and looking squarely at Creed as he defended himself.

"You want honesty? Here's some honesty for ya. Bring me what I want, or the girl don't make it home." Creed was done playing about.

"Don't hurt her," Billy said quickly. "I'll get what you need, and you leave Miss Emma alone. If you touch her, well, I don't expect to live, but you'd better know that you'll never be safe. The Hart brothers will hunt you down."

Creed's mouth pinched and his eyes narrowed. He glanced to Emma, then back to Billy.

"Why you still standing here, lookin' fit to cry, Billy-boy? *Miss* Emma here is counting on your chicken-heart to save her."

Emma wanted to slap Creed McCarty. She wanted to knock that nasty laugh right out of his mouth, but for once in her life she was choosing prudence. Maybe if she had chosen that path in the first place, she wouldn't be in this predicament at all.

"Miss Emma?" asked Billy.

She could see he was torn. He didn't know whether to leave and get back, or to stay and protect her. Emma wasn't sure either. She wasn't sure if Creed and Felix would keep to their word to leave her unharmed until Billy's return. Even if they did, what would happen to her once Billy came back? But she couldn't let Billy carry that guilt.

"It's okay. You had better do as they say," she replied.

The McCartys were outlaws. They lived only by the rules they made for themselves, and from what Wes had shared, and what Emma had now seen for herself, she wondered if she was even going to get out of this mess.

"Listen to the lady...you best git. Time's a tickin', Billy-boy. Time's a tickin'."

12
———

He should have left straight from the east pasture, but instead he turned Bass, back toward the Double H. He'd left a saddlebag at the bunkhouse and needed to retrieve it. When Early asked how he could have missed loading it, he claimed that it had just slipped his mind, but they both knew Wes was lying.

He couldn't seem to let go.

He'd found his time at the Double H refreshing, and the change of pace had been nice. As a marshal, Wes spent so much time alone, tracking outlaws or transporting felons, that he had almost forgotten what it was like to associate with good, decent people. His work left him jaded, but Wes was reminded that there were plenty of good people in the world, including a whole crew of them at the Double H. Yes, Wes liked it at the ranch, but that wasn't the reason he'd spent a week delaying the capture of the McCartys. No, that honor lay squarely with the opinionated, generous, confusing beauty that was Miss Emma Hart. She was an enigma, and he couldn't get enough.

Each time he swore it was the last time he'd see or speak

to her, his heart overruled his head, and he found himself marching right back to her. He'd spent more time milking cows and carrying wood to the kitchen, in hopes of even a glimpse of Emma. He was a poor excuse for a cowpoke, and not much of a lawman. If the Marshal's Office discovered he was spending more time on the trail of Emma Hart, going about her business at the Double H, than the men he'd actually been assigned, Wes would soon be out of a job, and rightly so.

Why was he bothering? No good could come from making Emma his own. They could try, and for a while they could be happy, but in the end, there would come a time, and the devil would take his due. He wasn't willing to risk that. Risk her.

As Wes reached the yard of the Double H, it seemed unusually quiet. Emma and Tilly were probably inside, and most of the men were off working their tasks for the day.

There was a rider coming in from the south, another horse, saddled but riderless, in tow. Instinct sent a prickle across his scalp and lifted the hair from the back of his neck. Something wasn't right.

Wes realized that the rider was Billy McCarty and the riderless horse Emma's Neptune, right about the same time. But where the blazes was Emma, and what was McCarty doing with her horse?

Urging Bass forward, Wes sped towards them.

He and Billy reached the stable at the same time. Wes jumped from his mustang and grabbed Neptune's reins, immediately checking the appaloosa for signs of injury.

Finding none, he turned to the pallid face of Billy, who was staring at him wide-eyed and terrified. Wes's gut tightened. He was right; whatever was going on was not good.

Wes grabbed Billy and pushed him up against the stable

boards. "What are you doing with Emma's horse? Where is she?"

The boy's jaw moved up and down, but no sound came out. Wes didn't have the patience or time for young McCarty's scared silence.

"Tell me what you know, Billy, or you and me are going to have a problem that's not so easily solved. What's happened? Where is Emma?" Lips pulled back and teeth bared, anger surged through him, and he wanted to shake the words from Billy.

"Please! Wes! I'm sorry," pleaded Billy.

"It's 'Marshal,' and tell me what you're sorry for, before I make you even more so," growled Wes.

"Marshal? What—?" Billy's face was a mixture of confusion and fear.

"Never mind that now. Talk."

"It's my uncles. They're—"

"I know who they are."

"They sent a messenger a few days back, asking me to meet 'em. I don't know how they found me. I wasn't going to, I swear I wasn't, but then I got another note saying they had news about my ma's family. I don't know why I believed 'em; it was stupid, but I went."

Wes growled and cursed the boy's proclivity for chatter. "I don't care about all that. Why is her horse wandering around here saddled, when she's nowhere in sight? How did you drag Emma into this mess?"

"It wasn't me!" Wes felt sick at Billy's answer, because he knew. He knew that Emma was in trouble.

He gripped the collar of Billy's shirt. "Where is she? Where's Emma?"

"I don't know why, but she followed me. They caught her. Creed found her spying and they took her. I couldn't stop 'em." Billy's shoulders slumped, no longer bothering to struggle against Wes's grip. "I told 'em I wouldn't do it, I didn't care what they did to me, but I wouldn't betray the boys here. But then he had Miss Emma. I couldn't stop 'em. Creed said if I brought him all the money from tossing the men's stuff here, he'd let her go."

Wes cursed, let go of Billy's shirt, and started to pace.

Billy dropped to the floor and started to cry. "I didn't want nothin' to do with them, I swear, Wes—Marshal, but they had Miss Emma, and then I couldn't say no anymore. I couldn't let 'em hurt her."

Wes swung back to face Billy. "Did Creed threaten her?"

"Yeah, but only if I didn't do like they wanted."

"Is she hurt? Did they hurt her, Billy? Was she okay when you last saw her?" Wes was shooting out questions like a gatling gun. His guts were in knots, and he wanted to be sick.

Billy looked up at Wes. "Last I saw, she was spitting mad, but she wasn't hurt." There was admiration in Billy's wet eyes as he spoke. "She never cowered, not once. She's the bravest gal I ever seen. She gave them as good as she got."

Wes squeezed his eyes shut against Billy's esteem. It was exactly as he feared. Emma had gone and tangled herself up in business she had no call messing with. She thought she could out-sass the McCartys, but men like that wouldn't put up with backtalk from anyone, much less a woman. They didn't deal in clever repartee. They dealt in bullets.

Billy was still talking. "I told 'em. I told 'em who she was, and that Harts would hunt 'em down to the end of their days if either one laid a hand on her." Billy swallowed. "Even if Creed and Felix let her go, I 'spect her brothers won't let this slide."

Wes took a deep breath and looked straight into Billy's wide eyes. "They're not the only ones."

He didn't need to formulate a plan; there was only one thing to do: go after Emma. Anything more could be decided on the ride. Wes didn't want to waste any more time than they already had.

Billy stood up. "What do you want me to do, Marshal?"

"Where are you supposed to meet them?" asked Wes.

"Over in Echo Gorge."

"Where is that?" he demanded.

"South. Head toward Berwick Mountain Range. If you follow the Battle River, it will lead you straight there. You'll know when you see the trees that look like two horseshoes. There's a reef of rock with a gap between 'em," explained Billy. "But I'm comin' with you."

Wes looked at Billy. "No, you're not."

Billy's face fell, and Wes knew that the young McCarty wanted to fix the mess that he'd helped make. "I ain't no coward, I swear. I ain't involved... I mean, I was... I am, but not like you're thinkin'. I want to help. You can trust me, Marshal."

Wes didn't have time to placate Billy and relieve the guilt he was feeling. "I get it, Billy, but I need you to do something else."

"Name it."

"I need you to ride out to the east pasture. That's where the Harts are now. You need to tell Gideon and the others everything."

"They'll kill me!" cried Billy, blanching.

"No, they won't. Tell them I sent you, and I'm headed for Emma." Wes watched as Billy blew out a breath that rattled his lips and nodded.

If the situation hadn't been so dire, Wes might have

laughed. "Go on. They won't hurt you. The Harts are better men than your uncles. Tell them what you told me, and where I'm going. I can't wait for them. It will take too long for you to get out there and for them to get back. I'm not letting them hold Emma for any longer than it takes."

"Yes, sir."

Billy didn't waste a minute. He was quickly mounted and headed for the east pasture. Wes had no doubt young McCarty would be terrified on his way there. He hoped his assessment of the Harts was correct and they wouldn't take out their fury at the news on Billy. He wasn't a bad kid—far from it—he was just a pawn in his uncles' game. Specifically, Creed McCarty's game. From all accounts, it was Creed who made the decisions for his brother. Wes was looking forward to seeing the woman-stealing coward get what he deserved.

With Billy gone, Wes kicked at a barrel and let out a roar of anger.

Calling to his horse, Wes counted his bullets and made sure his pistols were loaded. With Bass ready, he checked the shotgun in its sheath on his saddle and mounted. Jabbing his booted heels into the roan mustang's flanks, he took off. Trying to tamp down his worry, Wes instead found it joined by anger, and it wasn't only directed at the McCartys.

How could she have been so foolish? What in blazes had been running through her mind, that made her think going after Billy was a good idea? After everything he'd said, she hadn't listened to a word. Not one. Why couldn't she be passionate about cross-stitching and gardening, instead of seeking out trouble? What was she trying to prove? If anything, she had proven him right. This wasn't some adventure; this was real, and Emma could be hurt, or worse. Wes nearly choked on that last thought.

Hoping Billy's directions were sound, Wes leaned forward in the saddle, leaving the Double H Ranch behind him. It felt like the striking hooves of his trusty mount were echoing the pounding of his heart, and Bass could sense the urgency of his flight.

Alarm propelled Wes onward.

The farther he rode, the angrier Wes got, until he realized that it wasn't anger tying his stomach in knots. It was fear.

Wes had tracked, chased, and hunted many a ruthless man over the years. The McCartys were far from the worst, but never had he felt like this. He knew that he would find the McCartys, and they would pay for their crimes, but it was the fact that they were holding Emma captive that turned his rage hot and his fear cold.

He'd been after bad men before, but never had the stakes been so high.

EMMA WASN'T SPEAKING to her captors, and they seemed to be pleased with the arrangement. They kept to themselves, whispering occasionally when it was something they deemed important, but overall, the McCartys acted as though she didn't exist at all.

Felix had approached her a few times, but Creed called him away and set him on another task around their simple, makeshift camp. It was evident that Creed was calling the shots. Emma couldn't tell who was older, but Creed definitely made the rules.

From the quantity of empty tin cans and personal effects

strewn about, the brothers must have been staying here for the past several days, and by the information she gleaned from listening, the McCartys had thought that Billy would have been lured out days ago, but Billy wasn't interested. They had finally resorted to using his mother to get the boy to answer. They wanted him to bring whatever coins, cash, and valuables he could and then they would move on.

The plan seemed ridiculous to her, and the risk not worth the reward. If she were a bandit, she would have been long gone, not gambling on some estranged relative, but perhaps that just proved how desperate the McCartys really were.

Creed ordered Felix to tie Emma's hands behind her back. Using some dirty, old, hemp rope, Felix did as he was told, then shoved her against the trunk of a large tree, not bothering to secure her to it. Despite the alcohol fumes that oozed from the man's skin, Felix still managed to tie the knots tightly. Emma held back the insults that threatened on the tip of her tongue.

The McCartys puttered about the camp for a while. Then, with nothing but waiting to do, the two men pulled out some dried, leathery sticks of jerky, Felix adding more whiskey to his tin cup.

He looked over at her again. "Shouldn't we's be feedin' her, Creed?"

Creed narrowed his dark, cruel eyes at her as he responded to his brother. "No. Miss Fancy Lady don't need to be eatin' our vittles, Felix, so don't go givin' her none of yours."

"What's about water, Creed? Can I giv'er somma that?"

Emma watched as Creed's irritation grow. "Fine, give her some water."

Felix wandered over and offered Emma some water

from his canteen.

"As you can see, my hands are tied. Perhaps..." She lifted her shoulders and let her words trail off. Could she really be lucky enough to have them untie her?

Creed sent his nasty laugh her way. "Nice try."

Felix held up his canteen to her mouth and tried to pour it for her, but Emma pressed her lips together, disgusted by the filthy vessel and its matching owner. The man was repulsive. His long hair could have been any color beneath the dust, dirt, and grime that covered his head, and it was thick enough to hide the scarred flesh where his ear should be. Although he wasn't drinking, Creed wasn't much better. Emma doubted the men had had a recent bath, or maybe didn't even know what one was.

"Miss High and Mighty don't want nothin' from you, Felix," mocked Creed.

Felix leaned in. "I's only being nice."

Emma recoiled as the foul stench from his mouth reached her nose. She wrinkled her nose in disgust. Closing her eyes, she tried to recall the sweet smell of cinnamon that was Wes's breath, not the rotting teeth and firewater that was her reality.

"She's mean. I's don't wanna take her with us, Creed," pouted Felix, as he retreated to his seat by the fire.

Emma felt a brief flash of remorse, at hurting the simple man's feelings, as at least he'd attempted to be kind. Still, he was half of the duo that had taken her prisoner, and that fact helped lessen her guilt.

"We're not. Once Billy gets back, we'll turn her loose and get gone. I ain't afraid, but we don't need those Harts on our trail too."

Emma almost laughed out loud at Creed's mistaken belief. There was no way that her brothers would allow this insult to stand. The moment the McCartys took her, they had sealed their fate. Nothing would stop her brothers from hunting them down.

She would never be foolish enough to tell them that. Emma didn't want them to think there was no reason to keep her alive. So for now, she remained silent.

As the brothers talked to each other, Emma worked at the knots keeping her hands together. There were more than a few advantages to growing up with brothers, and the ability to loosen and unravel secured rope was one of them.

Like Gideon, Rhett, and Ben had done to them, Luke and Micah in turn had used their youngest sibling for roping practice. By the time that Emma was ten years old, she'd been hogtied so many times that she could undo any knot in her sleep. Her mother punished the boys the few times she caught them, but it was never from Emma tattling. She was just happy her brothers were including her in their games, and soon she was as proficient as they were.

It was getting cooler down in the gorge, and Emma was grateful she'd been wearing pants when she saw Billy ride off, rather than a dress. It also helped when they had thrust her into her uncomfortable position against the tree. She estimated that she'd been captive for about three hours, which ought to be enough time for Billy to ride to the Double H and be on his way back. Her mount should have made it home as well.

With everyone except Teresa and Tilly away from the ranch, Emma knew that if she didn't manage to free herself, her only way out of this predicament was for Billy to come through on whatever his uncles had asked him to do.

Emma looked over, trying to keep her loathing for the men from her face. She knew Billy would return, and she didn't doubt his desire to save her. The truth of the matter was, it wasn't Billy she had to count on. It was the McCarty brothers. And if she had to depend on the honesty and integrity of these two despicable outlaws, then she was in trouble. How long, before Creed realized taking her was a huge mistake? What would stop him from dispatching both her and Billy, leaving her family with, as he supposed, no evidence that the McCartys were even involved? They might figure it out in time, but the head start the McCartys would gain might appeal enough to Creed that he would think her disposal worthwhile. Even worse, he might take her with them, after killing poor Billy.

Emma knew she would prefer quick death to any extended time with Creed and Felix McCarty.

She sat and watched as her choices evaporated in her mind, one by one. Emma was going to have to save herself.

13

He was furious with Emma, but that soon gave way to guilt he placed on his own shoulders. Wes knew that if he had done his job properly from the get-go, Emma wouldn't even be in this predicament. He was to blame: no one else.

Pretending to be some ranch hand on the Double H had been a waste of time and a foolish ploy. He should have gotten the information he needed from Billy openly and followed the trail after Creed and Felix. If he'd done that, then none of this would be happening.

Blast it! Emma hadn't known a darn thing about the McCartys until he'd told her. Because of him, she'd mixed up adventure with unnecessary risk, and now—

No, he couldn't even think it.

Caught up in stealing glances and finding moments throughout his days to spend with Emma, he had lost sight of the job he'd been tasked to do. Stretching out each moment spent together, fighting his need to be near her, and the knowledge that he should be staying away, he craved time with Emma, and he had taken it. In return, he fell hard. Too hard.

Wes didn't believe in love at first sight, but love in a few days felt pretty real right about now. He'd fallen fast and hard for the tall, full-figured beauty. Her barely-contained zest for life frightened and thrilled him in equal measure. It was even the way she talked about seeing the ocean one day. She was excited about the world, and the opportunities it held. She hadn't been worn down by life.

Deep brown eyes and silky hair were only icing on the cake. Just the decoration, as Emma herself might say. It was the way her eyes flashed when she was arguing and the kind-hearted way she interacted with everyone working the ranch, with the clear exception of her teasing pack of brothers, that drew him in. In such a short period of time, Emma had found a way to break in, pulling down the bricks of his purposefully walled heart, and come marching in.

Well, he'd gotten what he wanted, time with Emma. But that time came with a price; Emma was paying the bill, and it was his fault.

He'd made too many mistakes, from the first moment they'd met. It was like he couldn't think straight, wasn't even himself since their introduction in Garvin's Mercantile. His commitment to his work had flown out the window and look what that had brought.

Emma deserved so much more than what he could offer. She needed to be protected, kept safe from the McCartys of the world. His job was to see that men like that were held accountable for their deeds, but Emma would be safer with her brothers. She would be sheltered at the Double H. Wes could make the world a safer place, but he could never share hers.

She needed to understand that.

Wes kept Bass at a steady canter. Fear and desire called on him to go faster, but instinct and experience told him not to wear out his mount. He didn't know if Emma and the McCartys would still be where Billy had left them, or if they had already departed. He had to prepare for any eventuality; anything could happen, but the final result was going to be the same. Wes would hunt down the McCartys, save Emma, and bring her safely home.

It was that simple; there was no other option.

Once that had been accomplished, Wes was going to get as far away from Autumn Springs, and Emma, as he could. He owed her and her brothers that much, at least.

Wes and Bass were going to ride until the vision of those deep brown eyes faded. Until he was in a place where no one had even heard of the Double H Ranch. Until his heart stopped aching and the memory of Miss Emma Hart finally disappeared.

BILLY STILL HADN'T ARRIVED, and Emma could tell that the McCartys were getting restless. Since he'd finished his meager meal, Creed hadn't stopped pacing about camp, muttering to himself and making both her and Felix nervous.

"Where in blazes is that boy?" yelled Creed.

No one answered. A response wasn't expected or required. Creed didn't want to hear from either of them; that much was clear. There were a few moments when he looked speculatively at her and Emma felt a shudder run through her. Creed had a gleam in his eye that said he might like to possess her, more than the money he was waiting on Billy to bring. Emma knew that if something prevented Billy from returning, Creed was going to take out his frustration and anger on her. She needed to be on her guard; she had no one else to count on right now.

Felix played with the small fire, throwing in bits of stick he found on the ground and watching as they burned. He rubbed often at his right shoulder, shrugging off his coat, to work the muscles that were bothering him. Emma was reminded of her own knots and continued to work at the ones that still bound her hands. She was so close, then suddenly they unraveled. Keeping the look of triumph from her face, she carefully rubbed her hands together, trying to stop the tingling as the circulation returned. Concealing her movements and her success, Emma kept her arms in position against the tree. She couldn't let them know she was free. Having her hands available was only half the battle. Getting away from the camp would be another matter entirely.

She considered her surroundings. There was a time when she had loved playing with her brothers in Echo Gorge, where their parents had taken them on family picnics. Battle River had plenty of fish, and it was normally a lovely spot.

Right now, Emma felt much different about the place.

Screaming and calling for help would make no difference. The canyon was in a secluded part of the Double H holdings. The same reason Emma loved this spot was the same reason she had no chance of assistance. Its solitary beauty and out of the way locale meant there was no one around. Anyone passing was probably trespassing and unlikely to help, lest they get themselves in trouble too.

Any attempt to make a run for it would also be met with failure. She was quick enough to have gotten Neptune on her way, but Creed or Felix could easily outrun her. She would have to come up with a better plan. She would only have one chance at escape. They wouldn't be so careless with her next time if she failed in her attempt.

Emma closed her eyes, forcing herself to think. It was too easy to sit here and hope that her brothers, or even Wes, would come riding in to save her. There was no way of knowing for sure that they even knew she'd been taken.

Watching the two men, Emma remembered a ridiculous fantasy she'd had when she was younger. She had thought that it might be romantic to be captured by some terrible but dashing outlaw in a stagecoach robbery, only to realize he wasn't a really a bandit, but a misunderstood hero. Robbing the rich to feed the poor, or something along those lines. He would declare his love for her, she would become Lady Bandit, and they would live happily ever after. She'd shared it with Nora, who was immediately horrified.

What a fool she had been.

She cringed at the memory. If Creed and Felix were any example, then Nora was right to be shocked. Emma was beginning to realize that there were many things she had romanticized, which in the real world were not only foolish, but downright dangerous.

But the recollection gave her an idea.

Emma's eyes darted back and forth between the brothers. She had been rude to Felix before, but maybe there was a way she could use him to her advantage. Perhaps if she played the role of helpless female, it might work in her favor. Maybe she could convince Felix to let her go.

Emma waited until he glanced her way, then gave him a tentative smile. His eyebrows squished together, and he scratched his temple. Felix looked to his brother. Emma's hopes were dashed. Felix didn't make any decisions for himself, and even if he wanted to, she couldn't picture him opposing his brother.

She continued to watch for an opportunity, almost giving up hope when she saw her chance.

Felix was sitting on an old tree stump, his dirty wool coat on the ground. Emma noticed that there was only one holster on Felix's gun belt, and he didn't have it tied down to his thigh. That was his first mistake. The second was the fact that he wore his holster cross-draw.

Carrying his iron butt-forward made sense for a man who probably spent a lot of time in the saddle. It was more comfortable and easier to reach when seated. If Felix's shoulder was bothering him, pulling across probably wouldn't irritate his injury as much. But it was far easier to take a gun off a man wearing cross.

Emma just needed him to get close enough.

Pretending to cough, Emma weakly cleared her throat, then attempted another smile in Felix's direction. He looked over, but he didn't look friendly.

"Mr. McCarty?" Emma watched as Felix straightened at her respectful address. "I know I was rude earlier. I think it's because I'm so scared. But now I'm so very thirsty, and I'm hoping you'll be kind enough to offer me some water from your canteen again."

She batted her eyes and gave her sweetest smile and saw that it was working. Felix was starting to soften.

They were interrupted by Creed.

"See! Real sweet now, ain't she? It's 'cuz she wants somethin'. Women are all the same." He sneered in her direction. "Usin' your feminine wiles to get what you want."

Emma didn't acknowledge Creed, or the fact that he was absolutely correct in his assessment of her. He didn't know it wasn't water that she wanted, and she aimed to keep it that way.

Felix tilted his head and narrowed his eyes on her. Emma watched as the little wheels in his mind turned and she continued to look as forlorn, sad and thirsty as she could. contShe even crossed her fingers behind her back. It was a pointless action, but she needed all the help she could get. All she wanted was to be free. She didn't need to bring the McCartys to justice. She doubted she could. Even if she had a gun, it was still two to one. If she let them ride off, she would live, and then Marshal Weston Hayes could go after them. He had all the time for it since he sure wasn't coming after her.

Emma let out a deep sigh and licked her parched lips. Her performance was enough to rouse Felix to action.

"She's just a lady, Creed. They's get scared real easy. I'm gonna give her some."

Creed spit on the ground. "I don't care, long as you quit talkin' about it. I'm getting the horses ready. Billy ain't coming back."

Emma held her breath as Felix got up, grabbed his canteen, and lumbered over to her by the tree. "Here."

Felix twisted the top off and bent down, leaning in to help Emma drink.

It was now or never.

Emma darted forward, pulling his gun from the holster, and kicked Felix, who, in his state of inebriation, sprawled backwards on the ground.

"Creed!" yelled Felix.

"Don't move!" shouted Emma. "Not one inch."

The gun felt heavy in her hand, but she recognized it as an old Colt single action army revolver. Her fathered carried one for a while, called it a 'smokewagon.' She sent up a thank you to her father, and Early, for having taught her how to use one. Revolvers weren't like rifles, but Emma knew how to use this one.

"Blazes, Felix, how'd you let a woman get the drop on you?"

Felix was about to reply, but Emma cut him off. "Stop talking, you brute." Feeling less helpless with the revolver in her hand, she dropped her sweet lady act. She was angry for so many reasons, and she was done playing nice.

Creed curled back his lip, sneering. "You ain't gonna shoot, little girl. That iron you're holdin' is a man's gun. You got no idea how to use it."

Emma cocked back the hammer, relaying an audible click, and with a steady hand pointed it at Felix. "Shall we find out? Are you a gambling man, Mr. McCarty? Willing to bet your brother's life?"

"Maybe," shrugged Creed. "The company ain't bad, but he's fair useless most times."

"Creed?" cried Felix.

The man was utterly despicable. Emma couldn't imagine being so careless with any one of her brothers' lives. He was the kind who only looked out for himself, never caring how his actions might affect others. He was the lowest of the low, and so Emma moved the bearing of Colt's barrel. It was now pointing directly at Creed, and his face dropped.

"How do you feel about yours?"

14

Wes crept down into Echo Gorge. Billy's directions had gotten him almost on top of the McCartys. He left Bass up top, then worked his way down, staying low and as quiet as he could.

Approaching the McCartys crude camp, he spied Emma tied up against a tree. She appeared unharmed, and Wes exhaled, releasing some of the fear he'd been holding in since he met Billy at the Double H.

He quickly noted the location of the McCartys horses, and then the terrain of the camp. Wes had only one shot at surprising the outlaws, and he couldn't afford to make a mistake. The costs this time around were too high. Emma's safety meant everything to him, and while he never wanted to be the sort of marshal who only brought in cold bodies, he found he didn't care if the McCartys didn't survive the day.

He wondered if Sheriff Wyley would throw an 'I told you so' his way. Funny, how the rules a man lived by could be tossed aside, when the woman he loved was in mortal danger.

Despite his frustration with Emma on the ride out, watching her now, he was impressed with her stoic appearance. Many a man would have crumbled under such conditions. She wasn't wailing or crying. Then again, from what had learned of Emma's character, that strength and resilience he had fallen so hard for, he probably shouldn't have expected anything less.

Wes's pulse quickened as he watched Felix get up from his seat and approach Emma. It looked like he was going to give her a drink from his canteen, when suddenly everything erupted.

From his vantage point Wes couldn't see what happened, but the tables were now turned, and Emma had a sizable pistol in her hands, pointed at Felix, who was now on his back, splayed out on the ground before her.

Then she shifted the gun to aim at Creed.

Wes moved quickly through the bush and stepped out between Creed and Felix, careful to stay out of Emma's line of fire.

"Wes!"

Her thrill at his appearance almost caused her to drop the gun, but she quickly refocused.

Creed growled. "Who in the blazes are you? One of them Harts?"

Wes didn't need to answer; Emma was already doing it for him. "He's Marshal Weston Hayes, and you, sir, are done."

She said it with such faith and satisfaction that Wes almost laughed, but now wasn't the time. Instead, he trained his gun on Creed and spoke slowly, lest the man misinterpret his demand. "Remove that gun from your holster and toss it on the ground. Do it real slow, McCarty, then stretch those arms high. I've got a bullet with your name on it if you feel like trying anything." Wes thought of what the man had done, taking Emma, and threatening her life. "Though, I almost hope you do. What kind of belly-crawler kidnaps a lady?"

Creed held up his hands. "Now, Marshal, don't go gettin' worked up. Me and Felix here ain't hurt her none. She was never even part of the plan. She stuck her nose where it don't belong. That's all."

Creed looked to Emma, down to Felix, and back to Wes. "And she ain't no lady. Look what she gone done to Felix. You ever seen a lady do that? 'Course, my brother ain't much of a man, if he's gonna let some little girl knock him 'round."

At his brother's words, Felix growled and launched himself at Emma's legs. The gun she'd been holding flew off behind her, and she went down, Felix pinning her to the ground.

Wes didn't have a choice; he had to protect Emma from Felix. Ignoring the sound of Creed's mocking laughter, Wes raced over to help her, not daring to shoot Felix in case he hit Emma instead.

He slammed the butt of his gun across Felix's skull and the outlaw's body immediately slumped. Wes threw him aside and, reaching down, pulled Emma into his arms.

"Emma!" He held her at arm's length, his eyes searching for any sign of injury.

"Wes!" Their eyes met, the knowledge of what could have happened passing between them. He wanted to hold her there forever, kiss her full lips until she swore she would never put herself in danger again, but he couldn't. He was here to help her, not to confuse her more. He had to remember that.

The sound of pounding hooves receding wrenched his attention from Emma. He had allowed himself to be distracted by her again. Creed McCarty was making his getaway!

With Bass out of reach at the top of the gorge, and McCarty with a clear head start, Wes knew what he had to do. He wasn't letting Creed get away, not after what he'd done to Emma.

"CREED!" Wes roared. He took a deep breath and lifted his arm.

Creed turned in the saddle, his face showing triumph at his escape. Wes's revolver unwavering, his resolve set, took aim. He was about to pull the trigger when Creed's horse, momentarily unguided, passed beneath the thick branch of a nearby tree. Creed struck it hard, nearly throwing him from his mount.

Creed slowly slid sideways from the saddle and tumbled heavily to the ground. The horse, happy to be relieved of its burden, stopped.

Emma gasped. Wes spun at the sound, thinking that Felix had come to, but it was only Emma, her hands clasped over her mouth. He felt awful. She must be horrified to witness such violence. The blow to Creed's head had been audible. He didn't feel sorry for McCarty, but he did regret that Emma had witnessed it. For all her talk, she was still a sheltered lady.

"I'm sorry, Emma."

She turned to Wes, her eyes sparkling. "Sorry? For what? That was brilliant. I thought you were going to shoot him, and I wouldn't have blamed you one bit, but that," Emma gestured at the fallen outlaw then clapped. "That was perfect."

Wes was utterly confused, but he wasn't surprised he was feeling that way. Nothing about Emma Hart was easy for him to understand. "He'll be out cold for a while. Can't say that's a problem for me."

Emma flashed a bright smile. "I agree! Go get him, while I find Felix's gun." Emma pointed to the motionless bandit beside her on the ground. "From that hit, and the whiskey, I don't think he's going anywhere anytime soon."

Wes gaped in disbelief.

Dirt on her shirt and grass stains across her pants, she was in a complete state of disarray, and she was smiling.

Smiling!

She saw him staring at her dishevelment. Her response was to smooth back her hair, removing a trapped twig, and lift her chin, while her brown eyes met his with all the dignity of a queen.

Admiration for her pluck rose. It also scared him. As far as Wes could tell, Emma ran headlong into everything. She had no moderation; there was not one lick of in-between with her. That might work for a young boy still trying to figure out his place in the world, but it was dangerous for a woman to behave in such a way.

A lot worse could have happened here today. There were a whole lot of what-ifs in this situation, and Emma had been fortunate it turned out the way it did. She got lucky. She needed to understand that.

"Why are you looking at me like that, Wes? We did it. Together. We won."

She was peering into his face with those big, innocent eyes. Was she really that oblivious to the jeopardy she'd been in? Could she really not understand what it was that scared him to death? That between her bold nature and his work, she could have died?

"Wes, what's wrong?" asked Emma.

Wes stared at her in disbelief, blinking slowly as she

stood there, waiting for him to answer. He didn't. Wes turned and strode out to Creed McCarty, still lying prone in the dirt. When the words finally did come, he threw them over his shoulder while he kept walking away. "You, Emma. What's wrong is you."

She made a brief squeaking sound, then the next thing he heard was most assuredly her mouth snapping shut. Wes didn't turn around to see her reaction to his hard words. He knew he'd hurt her feelings, but this time he didn't care.

For the first time since he'd met her, Emma Hart was at a loss for words, and Wes wasn't complaining.

THEY DIDN'T SPEAK as Wes roped and bound the McCarty brothers to their horses. Neither man had yet regained his senses, so there were no protests as Wes heaved them on, then joined their lines to Bass. Emma was glad they hadn't come to. She knew that a blistering lecture would be coming from Wes when he started talking, and she didn't want the McCartys privy to any of it.

Emma was almost working herself into a state with the conversation she was having with Wes, in her head. Based on assumptions, Emma was already mad at Wes for things he hadn't even said ... yet. He wouldn't be the only one with an opinion. Emma would have plenty to say too. By the time they began riding out of Echo Gorge and back towards the Double H, the sun was starting to set, but Emma's temper was still rising.

Without her own horse, Emma was obliged to share Bass with Wes, and while she would never admit it to him, she thoroughly enjoyed being nestled into the warmth of his body. When they started out, he had offered her his coat as well, but her pride refused it, not wanting to admit that she hadn't thought ahead when she'd torn off from the ranch after Billy. Wes would have used it as yet another argument in the lecture she knew she'd be hearing soon enough. She didn't regret her refusal at all, since as the air cooled, Wes pulled her in closer, blocking the wind and protecting her with his body.

Emma wished he would talk. Silence might be what he needed, but it was killing her with every plodding step the horses took. She hated waiting, feeling like the axe was about to fall. Emma preferred an upfront battle to a siege of silence. She wasn't one to avoid confrontation of any kind.

Tipping back her head, she looked up to Wes. "Are you going to stay silent the whole ride?"

Wes didn't respond.

Emma blew out a long breath. He was stubborn and pig-headed and those were two attributes that were not on her list to check off. She was starting to think he was more like Gideon than she'd like.

She tried again. "You're going to have to say something, at some point. Otherwise, I might as well be riding with one of the McCartys back there."

That got him. "Let me know which one you'd prefer."

"Ah! He speaks."

Emma felt Wes's body stiffen, and she knew she was about to get an earful.

"Talk," growled Wes. She could feel the rumble against her back as he spoke. "You want talk? Fine. I'll talk, you listen."

"What were you thinking? What on earth possessed you to ride out after Billy? I thought you were bold before, but I think I've changed my mind. You're not bold, Emma Hart, you're reckless. And while you might, in some twisted way, take that as a compliment, I assure you I do not mean it as such. You acted without thinking about the consequences of your actions." Wes was fired up now. "Did you even consider what you put poor Billy through? He could have told his uncles no, walked away, and let your brothers or the sheriff know that they had approached him. Instead, he blames himself for you getting caught, and to save you, he thought he'd have to steal from his friends. That boy has fought his whole life *not* to be a criminal, and despite the odds, he'd succeeded. Until you decided to play lawman."

It was Emma's turn for silence. What could she say? Her lashes were wet with tears, but Wes wasn't done.

"You wanted me to talk, Emma, well, there you go. I won't even start with the panic I'm sure your brothers are feeling right now. They are headed out this way, not knowing if their sister is alive or dead. And I assure you, that kind of ride is one no man should have to take."

Wes's voice cracked with his final words, and that's when Emma knew it was more than anger he'd been feeling; it was fear too.

She'd anticipated a lecture, but that didn't lessen the sting of each truth he spoke. It was made all the more painful because she knew he was right. It was one thing to read or dream about the exciting life of a dime-novel hero, it was another to live out the realities of one. Wes was an actual deputy US marshal, with all the experience that came along with the title. He'd tried to warn her, but she hadn't listened.

Emma was listening now, and she wanted him to know that she had learned a valuable lesson. She also didn't want him to be angry with her anymore. The frustration she had felt earlier was long gone; she couldn't fault Wes for what he felt.

"I'm sorry." It started as a whisper, but then Emma cleared her throat and said it louder. "I'm so sorry, Wes. You're right. I didn't think about the position I'd put others in, and how they might feel."

She felt Wes's shoulders drop, the anger leaving his body. "It's the position you put yourself in too, Emma."

Hoping to make him laugh, Emma replied, "I thought you could at least congratulate me for getting free and not getting myself killed."

Wes groaned and pressed his mouth against the back of her head before he spoke. "Don't even jest, Emma. There is not one moment of this that is funny. The idea that you...I can't."

Emma felt the hurt and concern in his voice. "I'm sorry. I shouldn't make light of it, any of it. I think I do that sometimes when I don't know what to say, or I'm scared."

She shivered, and Wes held her close. "You don't have to be scared anymore, Emma, I've got you." His lips pressed against her hair as he said it again. "You're safe. I've got you."

"I feel safe, here in your arms, Wes."

His body stiffened. Emma didn't understand what she had said that could make him react that way. "What's wrong? Is it so terrible that I feel safe with you?"

He didn't respond, but Emma felt him trying to find the words to say.

"I know I just gave you an earful, Emma, and I meant it, but I'm also to blame. If it hadn't been for me, for the work I do, for who I am, you wouldn't even be in this position."

"What do you mean? The fact you're a marshal doesn't put me in danger, Wes. There are plenty of lawmen out there with wives and families."

"There are plenty of fools." His tone was harsh. When

Emma questioned him, he hesitated, then began to relate the awful events of the night he lost his mother.

Emma's heart ached for the little boy Wes had been, scared out of his wits, watching his whole world fall apart. She could see why he had decided to dedicate his life to the law, not understanding that there could be a path to both family and his work. Wes only had his own experience to draw from; he didn't know anything else. She pressed her hand to his, wanting him to know that she understood. His fingers interlaced with hers.

She wondered if he had even considered that there could be another way.

"Would you ever want a family?" asked Emma.

"A family is not for me."

"That's not an answer to my question."

Wes sighed. "I can't answer the question you're asking, Emma. I don't want to hurt you."

"Why can't you answer? Is it because you don't want something like that with me?"

"No! No, that's not it at all. I would lov—it doesn't matter, I won't ever let what happened today, happen again. I won't see you hurt, or worse. I couldn't bear it." Wes gripped the reins tightly, but Bass shook off the pressure with a snort, and Wes relaxed.

"You don't understand. When Billy told me ..." Wes's voice cracked. "When I knew that the McCartys had taken you, I thought I might explode with rage. But it wasn't all rage, Emma. It was fear. Fear that something might happen to you and guilt that I hadn't been strong enough to walk away from you, in order to keep you safe. I messed up. I put the one person I cared for in harm's way, because of my own selfish desires. What kind of man does that, Emma? You tell me, what kind of man?"

His voice was choked with pain, and Emma wished they weren't riding, so she could hold him in her arms and offer the same comfort that she felt in his embrace.

"That is not true, Wes. You're blaming yourself for things that aren't your fault." Emma tried to reassure him. "You're a good man. One of the finest I've ever met. You aren't only one thing. You're not just a lawman, at the expense of all else. I've watched you with Tilly. You would be a wonderful father."

"Stop. Please stop," he beseeched her.

Emma wasn't giving up. "I don't want you to walk away from me, Wes. I don't want you to walk away from a chance at a full life. You deserve that, and so do I. Danger isn't just in your job. It's everywhere. This land out here could take any one of us, at any time. My own family is proof of that. Sickness, accident, and yes, even murder, are the realities of the world we live in here in the territory and I don't imagine it's much different anywhere else."

He didn't respond, so she continued. "If we live our lives in fear, then is that really living? All I'm asking is that you allow your heart to be as courageous in life as it is in law."

"Your words make it sound easy, but it's not that simple, Emma," said Wes.

"It can be."

She let the silence fall between them again. She didn't want to argue, and she didn't know what else to say. Maybe Wes needed time to take in what she had said to him, and in turn, to believe it could be true.

As they headed back to the Double H, Emma wondered if her brothers would already be there or if they would meet them on the way. She felt awful, knowing that until they saw her, they would be worried sick. She couldn't even imagine how frightened she would be if the tables were turned, and it was one of her brothers who had been taken by outlaws. They were going to be furious, but Emma hoped their relief at seeing her safe might dull their anger.

As the sun sank toward the horizon, Emma found the exhaustion of her experience catching up with her. As brave as she wanted to be, the events of the day had still taken their toll. It was getting harder to stay awake, and it felt so good to have Wes holding her close.

Bass's steady gait was like water over river stones, and soon the rhythmic beating of Wes's heart and the warmth of his body lulled her to sleep.

15

Emotions he couldn't name swept through Wes as he felt the gentle curves of Emma's body relax into his as she gave in to sleep. Even though she had been so strong through it all, Wes was surprised she'd stayed awake as long as she had. He didn't blame her. He knew when he made it back to Mrs. Durnford's tonight that he would be asleep before his head hit the pillow.

Her body fit so perfectly against his. Wes knew he shouldn't think about it. It would lead nowhere. He had to be content that, for now, he was able to provide the comfort she needed, and when the time came, he would return her to the loving arms of her family.

No matter what he felt, he couldn't act on it.

He needed to take the McCartys in to Autumn Springs and leave them with the sheriff. Maybe get a doctor to look at the brothers, since neither one had made a peep since they'd been knocked out. It made for an easy trip, but Wes still wanted them healthy enough to face the justice they had coming.

Bass's ears pricked up, and soon Wes could hear it too.

The thundering sound of hooves reached them before he could see any riders. Given the direction the noise was coming from, it was no surprise when all four Hart brothers and a posse of Double H men came into sight.

He should have felt relief knowing that Emma would be safe with her family, and that he could get on with bringing in the McCartys, but he didn't. If Wes thought that holding on was hard, that was nothing to the pain at the thought of letting go.

He gave Emma a little nudge as her brothers approached. She woke and sat up straight, cool air filling the space where she had been. It left him feeling more than chilled; it left him feeling empty. His time with Emma had truly ended, and despite the warning he had given himself, Wes still hadn't expected it to hurt this much.

"Emma!" shouted Ben, his horse the first to reach them.

Pulling her from Wes's mount, he enveloped his little sister in his huge embrace, crushing her to his chest. Emma nearly disappeared in his arms.

"Thank goodness you're all right." Ben looked her over. "You are okay, right?"

"I am. Thanks to Wes—Marshal Hayes," replied Emma, as she wiped a tear that escaped at her brother's welcome.

"Good. 'Cuz Gideon's going to kill you."

"No, I'm not," said Gideon. He dismounted and came over to hug his sister in turn. "I'm just relieved you're okay." Then he walked over to shake Wes's hand. "I don't know how we can thank you, Marshal."

Wes took the proffered hand but shook his head all the same. "Not sure there's much to thank me for. If it weren't for my presence at the Double H, Miss Emma never would have gotten into this mess." He glanced over to where Emma was now being enfolded in Rhett's arms.

"To her credit, she did a fair job of getting out of it herself."

Luke came over, and Wes got off his horse. If Emma's brother had wanted to take a slug at him for his part in all this, Wes wouldn't stop him.

Instead, Luke extended his hand. "All of us here know Emma well enough to know that she's of her own mind. What you, or any of us, do or say don't usually make much difference." Luke smiled at Wes. "So, thank you for bringing my sister back. You're not as bad as I first thought."

Wes chuckled and took Luke's hand. Luke continued, grinning. "You know they say it takes a big man to admit when he's wrong about something, Marshal."

"I'm not sure if you're complimenting me or yourself, *Mr. Hart*," Wes winked as he said Luke's name.

Laughing, Luke shrugged. "Can't it be both?"

Wes returned the grin. "I guess it can."

He liked these men, and he'd have fond memories of the time he'd spent at the Double H. They were all good people with good hearts. He was amazed they were able to forgive his part in things, although Wilson Booker was not looking impressed, on the back of his horse. He was a hard nut to crack, and Wes didn't begrudge him his opinions.

Emma would be safe here. She would be loved and protected, and that was all he wanted for her.

"Are they dead?" asked Gideon, cocking his head toward the trussed McCartys, draped over their horses.

Rhett had gone over to inspect the men. Bending down to pull up an eyelid and peer into Creed's eye, he looked up with a grin. "Nope, but I don't expect they'll be up anytime soon."

"They're still breathing." It wasn't a question, but Gideon appeared genuinely surprised.

Luke shook his head upon hearing the news. "Seems to me those men got lucky it was you who reached them first, Marshal."

Booker nodded at Luke's words.

Wes didn't agree. "I don't dispense the justice, Luke, I'm only here to see that it has a chance to be served." He smiled. "Somehow, knowing how the situation went down, I don't think any of you boys would have done any different."

Gideon tipped his head slightly to one side, tugging on his ear. "Maybe. Maybe not." He gave his sister another hug, and then swung up on his horse. "I'll ride with you to Autumn Springs. No point in added risk when they do come to."

Wes nodded. "I'd appreciate the company."

They were about to leave when Emma called out. "Wes!"

She started to walk towards him, then stopped. Wes knew then that he'd never seen a more beautiful woman than Miss Emma Hart, nor would he ever again. He waited for her to speak.

"Will you be coming back with Gideon?"

He knew the question she was asking. The hope, clear in those big brown eyes, almost broke him right there. He shook his head. It was time to do the right thing. "No, I'll be riding on once the McCartys are with the sheriff."

"Oh." It was only one word, and it came out as a whisper, but it conveyed so much more. Her shoulders sagged. "Well, thank you...Marshal." She hesitated a moment longer but must have realized that there was nothing more to say. "Goodbye."

Wes simply touched his fingers to the edge of his hat, the same fingers that had so recently intertwined with hers. Then he pulled down the brim, sheltering his face, needing to hide the longing that was evident there. He didn't trust himself to speak, so he said nothing, knowing that look of hurt and disappointment on her face would be seared on his soul, forever.

Giving Bass a nudge, Wes joined Gideon and headed to town. He didn't dare look back; he might not have left if he had. It would have to be enough to know that she was where she needed to be, safe in the bosom of her family.

~

EMMA WAS NOT GOING to cry.

Not after all that had happened, not out here in the open, not in front of her brothers.

Ben came up and put his arm around her, pulling her close. He opened his mouth to comfort her, but Emma shook him off, speaking softly. "Not here. Not now. Please."

She kept blinking, hoping it would keep her tears at bay. She was made of stronger stuff than to fall apart because a man didn't want her, or worse, didn't think her heart worth the effort. At least she would be strong enough not to do it in front of him.

With Wes and Gideon gone, Emma and the rest of the men journeyed back to the Double H. Her time away had been short, but it made her appreciate her home all the more. Teresa and Mendo were waiting out in the yard, and when Luke helped Emma down from his horse, Emma ran to Teresa's waiting arms.

The men left to tend their horses and Teresa brought Emma back into the main house. Tilly had been put to bed, unaware of the situation. Gideon hadn't wanted his daughter frightened, and until they knew what they were dealing with, he wanted her kept in the dark.

Emma was thankful for the decision, as she couldn't

imagine trying to answer the insatiable curiosity of a child's questions right now. If there was one thing she had learned, and that left no room for doubt, it was that not all adventures were created equal. It would be a lesson she would also need to impart to Tilly.

Teresa prepared a bath, and Emma gratefully sank beneath the water, washing away the memory of the day. There was nothing more she wanted than to forget about this day and slide between the clean sheets of her bed, and pretend her heart wasn't broken.

She wasn't that lucky.

After she finished bathing, her brothers asked her to meet them in the big room and relate the events of the day. To their credit, they didn't lecture or badger her, not even Gideon, as she had expected. They could see she was exhausted and knew she would probably have more to say in the morning.

Emma was happy to put off any further conversation. Her bed was calling, and her heart was aching, the combination making it so she could barely keep her eyes open.

She soon drifted off to sleep with a wet pillow, a heavy heart, and the vision of Weston Hayes riding out of her life.

16

Wes made his way from the widow Durnford's down to the sheriff's office. His night had been a restless one, his thoughts swirling like an eddy in the river, with Emma the reason they churned. He hurried; he had slept in later than planned and he needed to finalize some papers with Sheriff Wyley before he could officially leave the McCartys in the sheriff's care and collect on his contract.

As he walked, Wes ran over last night's conversation with Gideon on the ride in. Emma's brother had asked him to keep Emma and her captivity from his report. Gideon knew he could count on silence from the men of the Double H and was hoping that the McCartys would keep their mouths shut, not wanting to add to their already foot-long list of offenses.

It didn't matter to Wes. The end result for the McCartys would be the same whether they were charged for taking Emma hostage or not. Gideon feared for his sister's reputation if the whole story ever came out. Wes readily agreed to his request. He would have done anything to make things easier for her.

Gideon also asked if Wes was planning on coming back to Autumn Springs. Emma's brother was no fool. He had seen their emotionally charged goodbye, but he didn't question Wes further.

Gideon accepted his negative answer, agreeing that it was for the best, and added that it was better that Wes left now. " It's never good when things are one-sided."

His odd reply left Wes believing that Emma's brother wasn't talking about them, but something or someone else, but as they approached town, both men had tacitly agreed to drop the subject.

When they arrived at the sheriff's, Gideon helped Wes unload the McCartys while Sheriff Wyley sent for the doctor. By the time the sheriff had returned with Doc Owens, Gideon was already headed back to the Double H, and Wes's time with the Harts was at an end.

Now pausing just inside the door to let his eyes adjust to the dim morning light of the sheriff's office, Wes nodded to Sheriff Wyley, who was looking entirely too lively for a man who'd been woken from his slumber last night.

"Morning, Sheriff," acknowledged Wes, as he rubbed his eyes.

"You don't look like you got much rest. I would have thought you'd be sawing logs all night after you took off from here," replied the sheriff.

"You and me both," said Wes.

"Hope I didn't steer you wrong with Mrs. Durnford's place."

Wes smiled at the sheriff's mention of the widow. The lawman could find a way to fit her into almost any conversation.

"Not at all. Exactly as promised. Clean sheets and thick walls. It was my mind that wouldn't quiet," explained Wes.

Wyley looked across at him, his fingers fiddling with, then twisting the long ends of his mustache. "I've had a night or two like that myself ... I've a good ear, if you've a mind to talk."

It was a genuine offer, but Wes couldn't turn down a chance to tease the man. "That an observation from Mrs. Durnford, Sheriff?"

Both the sheriff's good ears turned red beneath his white hat. "I'm retracting that offer."

Wes chuckled at the lawman's response. "I'm only here to check on the McCartys and finish up our paperwork."

"As you can see, they are doing just fine. You left before he finished his once-over, but Doc Owens said a good thump to the head never did anyone any harm." The sheriff shrugged. "Can't say I'm convinced that man even knows what he's talking about half the time, but where these boys are headed, I don't think they'll need to worry about all that."

Wes checked out the two men glaring at him from the cells behind the sheriff. Their eyes were shooting daggers, but their mouths were silent. Probably on account of the rags that had been stuffed in their mouths. Their hands were tied behind their backs.

Amused, Wes looked back to Sheriff Wyley, one eyebrow raised. "You allowed to do that?"

"You know a law says I can't?" The sheriff retorted. "I warned 'em. Both of 'em. First, I separated them, but it didn't stop the yelling and the fighting. Kept yappin' at each other through the bars."

Sheriff Wyley leaned forward to continue in the tones of

a theater-show narrator. "Seems the one with the whistle tooth—"

"Felix?"

"Yeah, him. Seems he doesn't take too kindly to his brother's intention to leave him behind and save his own skin. Been real sensitive about the whole thing." He chuckled. "Lotta hurt feelings back there, Marshal. 'Cept, that one." He jabbed his thumb in Creed's direction. "That one ain't got any."

Wes grunted his agreement.

"I may be an old man, but I still hear fine, and those two made too much noise. And now they don't."

The sheriff looked quite pleased with himself, and Wes couldn't disagree. He and Gideon had been lucky not to hear a peep from either brother as they brought them in. There had been plenty of other times when complaining, cursing, even pleading felons nearly drove him crazy on a long ride. But the sheriff looked entirely too satisfied, so Wes thought he'd give him a little poke.

"I thought you said you were a good listener. Or is that only for a select few?" teased Wes.

"I see. You think you're a funny one."

"Naw, just observant, Sheriff. Just observant."

Wyley snorted, then moved on. "What are your plans now? Circuit judge will be here soon, and these fellas will have their fates decided. You got another paper in that marshal's pocket to chase after?"

"Not yet. I'll be heading back to the Marshal's Office in a few weeks; might take my time in getting there. Need to clear my head a bit."

Wyley nodded. "You ever think of trading in that federal badge for something more local?"

Wes didn't know what the sheriff was getting at, but the

last thing he planned on doing was sticking around Autumn Springs. Knowing Emma existed, without being with her, would be hard enough, but regularly seeing her around town while keeping apart would be unbearable.

"Why do you ask? You considering taking off that badge so you can court Mrs. Durnford?"

"I don't need to remove my star to do that; I ain't looking to retire."

The sheriff got up and opened the door. "Come. Sit with me, Marshal."

Wes followed the man outside and they settled into the two chairs by the bench against the wall of the jail.

Sheriff Wyley lit a cigarillo and offered one to Wes, who declined.

"Not too early in the day for that?" asked Wes.

The sheriff inhaled, then let out a contented sigh. "It's never too soon to do the things you enjoy, son. Keep putting things off, and one day you'll wake up, and find it's too late. Opportunity will have passed you by."

"You still talking about smoke, or referring to the lovely widow Durnford, Sheriff?"

The sheriff exhaled another smoke cloud and Wes pulled a cinnamon candy from the bag in his pocket. He sucked on it to try and balance the smell.

"Both," chuckled the sheriff. "And since you aren't letting it go, I'll let you in on a little secret about Mrs. Durnford and I."

Wes had a feeling that the sheriff's 'secret' was well known to most of Autumn Springs. "Let me guess, you're sweet on her."

Sheriff Wyley let out a laugh that came straight from his belly. "Sweet doesn't even begin to cover it, Marshal."

He patted the upper left pocket in the vest, beneath his

coat. "I've been carrying this around, waiting for the right time."

"I thought you said we shouldn't hold off on—"

"I know what I said, but I'm not sure she's willing to give up that boarding house just yet. I think she likes the freedom it provides."

Wes didn't understand. "I would think that cooking and caring for one man would be preferable to a house full of strangers."

The sheriff scoffed. "Then you don't know much about women."

Wes wasn't going to argue with that.

Wyley rolled the cigarillo to the right side of his mouth, chewing on it before he continued. "She didn't have it easy with Morris Durnford, so she's not looking to give up what she only just found."

"And you? You're willing to give up the office of Sheriff for her?" asked Wes.

"That's twice now you've said that," said the lawman irritably. "What makes you think I need to retire, if I want to make that woman my wife?" The sheriff briefly glanced at Wes, then back out to the street before them. "There, yeah, I said it."

"You can't really be considering marrying Mrs. Durnford *and* staying sheriff?" Wes was shocked at how casual Sheriff Wyley was about the entire thing.

"'Course I can. Why not?"

The sheriff was looking at him like he'd lost his mind, but Wes wasn't about to explain his family history to the man.

"Aren't you worried that your line of work will put her in danger?"

It seemed pretty clear to Wes. If the past twenty-four

hours were proof of anything, they were that he'd been right to be wary of combining love and the law.

"Being the sheriff of Autumn Springs? Nope, can't say's I am." The sheriff shook his head. "We may have the occasional outlaw coming through, or the ones your office brings us, but Autumn Springs ain't exactly riddled with menace. It's a pretty safe place to lay your head, Marshal."

"Anything is possible, Sheriff."

"Well sure, but the bigger fears 'round here come with the realities of living in a new land, and everyday life. We had a fever come through here a few years back, took a lot of good people with it. Mining accidents, stock mishaps, even storms take more lives than what you're talking about." Sheriff Wyley shrugged. "Anything can happen, at any time. Guess that's why we live the way we do. Enjoy the moments we can."

"What do you mean?" asked Wes.

"Marry quick and love hard; we don't all have the luxury of time. There's no guarantees in this world."

His words rang true, and they made sense, but thinking one way for so long made it hard to imagine anything other than what he'd grown up believing.

"You don't worry at all?"

"I worry about plenty. Some real, some just things I've made up in my head."

"I don't know, Sheriff. I've seen firsthand the pain that kind of loving can bring," said Wes.

"I'm sorry for your hurt, son, but let me tell you this. It can make you realize how lucky you were for what you had and show you what you've taken for granted. If you ain't ever felt pain, how can you truly experience the totality of joy? Now, I'm not saying I wish that kind of ache on anyone. But it's darn near impossible to make it through life without some kind of hurt, no matter how hard you try. You might as well take the good too."

Wes scuffed the heel of his boot against the wooden planks of the boardwalk, tracing lines in the dust. "I just don't know, Sheriff."

"No one does. But I'm just an old man rambling on. The reason I brought you out here, was I wanted to offer you a job."

"A job? I've got one, and you said you weren't retiring."

"I'm not ... yet. But that time's not too far off, and right now I need a deputy."

"Isn't Sheriff an elected position? If you stepped down later, I would have to run for office. I don't know if that is for me. It's tough enough one-on-one; I'm not sure I could convince a whole town to back me." Wes couldn't picture himself giving speeches and buying drinks to win favor.

"With the Harts in your corner, it'd be a shoo-in. I could see the respect Gideon Hart had for you, and he's not one to impress easily. But as I said, I ain't retiring yet. Don't get ahead of yourself."

At the mention of the Harts, the heavy feeling in his stomach returned.

Wes was planning on leaving Autumn Springs, not making the town his home. Even if he believed the sheriff was right about it all, he'd already walked away from Emma, twice. Surely, she wasn't going to forgive that.

He couldn't stay here, working next to Sheriff Wyley, waiting for the day that Emma came riding down Main Street, a wagon full of young ones, looking just like their momma. Not if they weren't his.

The very thought made him sick. Emma married, loving another man, was not acceptable.

"I'm not sure what to say, Sheriff," said Wes.

"I don't need an answer right now. Just think on it," he replied.

Wes let out a long sigh. *Think on it.* He'd be doing nothing else. But the old sheriff had put a burr in his saddle, and Wes wasn't going to be able to do anything else until he worked it out.

He held out his bag of candy, offering the sheriff one. Crunching the one he'd been sucking on between his back teeth, he tossed another in his mouth. Good thing he had a full bag.

Wes had some pondering to do.

USING AN OLD RAG, Emma brushed the dust off the top of the old cedar chest in the corner of her room. It had been too long since she had last looked inside.

The hope chest had belonged to her mother and survived her journey west to the untamed land where Emma's parents hoped to build their new lives. The leather straps and tabs, though dusty, were still in good repair, and the iron locks and edge clamps had thus far managed to avoid a rusty fate. It wasn't fancy, painted, or carved with intricate design. It was solid construction, meant to weather life's adventures, not designed as a parlor ornament. But it held the memories of her mother, and Emma loved it well for that reason alone.

When her heart ached, Emma longed for her mother's reassurances and since her death, the only maternal comforts she had were the reminders of Elizabeth Hart that lay within. With Wes gone and no one to turn to, Emma sought the contents of the chest.

The top box held her mother's old pieces of jewelry and

homemade gifts from her six children. Beneath that, carefully tucked away, was the light blue challis gown her mother had worn on her wedding day. Emma lifted it from the chest with reverence and held it to her nose, hoping that it would still carry her mother's scent.

The dress had an unpretentious design, with a minimal bustle and narrow waist. Lace her grandmother had knit adorned the edges of the three-quarters length sleeves. The neckline had a humble ruffle of the same lace. Simple, yet beautiful, just like her mother. She could recall her father calling from another room, "It would have only been gilding the lily" when her mother noted the simplicity of the dress while showing it to Emma one day.

After convincing her mother to put the dress on, young Emma was certain she must have been some sort of secret princess. Emma's adoring eyes only saw the smiling woman who loved and cared for their family, so elegant in the fine garment, and Emma never noticed how the bodice panels no longer laced tightly together until her mother had pointed it out. Even after six children, Elizabeth Hart had been beautiful.

Whimsy suddenly struck and, after checking the clock atop her dresser to be sure that Tilly should be resting for a little while longer, Emma decided to put the gown on.

After donning the dress, fastening and tightening to the best of her abilities, Emma took her brush and went after her hair, coiling it, then pinning her brown tresses in place. She mentally thanked her brothers for the long mirror that they had gifted her one Christmas, as she wasn't confident enough to leave her room in the dress, just yet. She hesitated, not daring to look. Then, gathering her courage, she went to stand before the mirror.

She looked...she looked like her mother.

Emma raised her fingers and touched her hair, so similar to her mother's. Her mother certainly had more of the grace required to achieve the formal look, but for once, Emma didn't feel she was lacking.

But the respite was brief, and, despite her best efforts to feel otherwise, and as lovely as the dress was, Emma felt decidedly...inadequate.

What was wrong with her? Why hadn't Wes even tried to find a solution? His words and his actions were so confusing. When he had confessed his fears, and Emma understood his concerns, she was certain they could have found a way to be together, if only he had been willing to try.

The only thing that could explain his decision was that he really didn't feel the same as she did, and that he needed an excuse to leave. With her actions yesterday, she had provided a ready one.

Emma hated feeling like she needed to change in order to be loved. Why couldn't she be accepted for who she was, and not reprimanded for what she wasn't? It often felt like people believed she expected too much, that her circumstances allowed her to be too picky, and that spending all her time with her brothers had left her lacking as a woman.

Perhaps she was picky, but Emma didn't want to settle. She wouldn't settle.

At least she could take comfort in knowing that she would always have a place to call home. Other women had fared far worse.

If she couldn't have a husband and family of her own, she could live out her days as the spinster of the Double H Ranch, attending to the children her brothers might have and becoming as dour as Gideon. There were times when he would laugh and smile, but since his heart seemed to have died with her those times were few and far between.

Emma and Gideon could be two peas in a pod. A pod of disappointment.

Then she let out a laugh, followed by a heavy sigh, and lay back on her bed.

If word got out in Autumn Springs that she had spent hours alone in the company of the McCartys, she wouldn't have a suitor from among even the least of the town's candidates. Her brothers would, of course, close ranks to protect her, as they had said they would last night, but even the Hart name might not be enough to silence the wagging tongues of the town. Her family was well-liked and respected, but there were always those who reveled in the downfall of others.

It was so unfair. In her opinion, the McCartys had proven themselves to be rather useless criminals, and they hadn't done her any serious injury. Her arm was still sore from where Creed had grabbed her, and hip sore from when Felix tackled her, but overall—considering what could have been—she had fared quite well.

Maybe Wes couldn't see that. He seemed to think that being taken should have been traumatic for her, and while he admitted a grudging admiration for her daring escape attempt, he still refused to see reason.

Women's reputations were so fragile. Any one of her brothers could have spent days being held by bandits, and they would only be celebrated for their bravery in getting away. Maybe even a town parade for the capturing the outlaws as well. Men never had to worry about these things. They could walk around doing whatever they wanted, and nobody would say a thing.

Even break a heart.

Emma wanted to scream, then she wanted to cry. How was she supposed to carry on when all she could think about was Marshal Weston Hayes? And how could she continue to love someone who, right now, she wasn't even sure she liked?

Yes, she had made a foolish choice in following Billy, but wasn't being held hostage by those despicable men punishment enough? Emma had learned a valuable lesson. There was a huge difference between enjoying an adventure and endangering oneself unnecessarily. Why couldn't Wes see that?

Sitting up, Emma stared at her reflection in the mirror while she sat on the bed. She did look like her mother. What would her mother have told her to do?

Emma would have to accept that a life with Wes was not the life planned for her. There must be a different path for her, and in time it would reveal itself. Elizabeth Hart had been a smart, strong woman, and that's what she would want her daughter to be. But she had also been a warm and tender mother, and so perhaps she wouldn't mind if, for a little while, Emma allowed some tears to fall before she stepped through her bedroom door and pretended that her heart wasn't shattered and that lie became the truth.

There was a knock at her bedroom door.

17

"Emma?" It was Gideon.

The last thing she wanted was another lecture from her eldest brother, telling her that it was for the best, that she didn't need to be mooning over a man who wasn't willing to fight for her. Last night's sermon had been enough. Gideon had been adamant that one-sided love was a fool's game, and he didn't care that she was certain Wes cared for her too. He said that if Wes truly loved her, he'd be here, and he wasn't. Gideon warned her that Wes's actions spoke for themselves, and she would be better off forgetting all about him. Emma had no idea what had soured Gideon so thoroughly on love; it couldn't just be his grief for Cordelia. Either way, he believed what he did, and she wasn't going to try and change his mind.

"Go away, Gideon. I have nothing to say to you, and I think you made yourself clear last night." She sighed. "You all did." It wasn't even that she was angry anymore. She was sad, and she was tired, and she wished that she had the power to change things, but she did not, and that was that.

"Don't be stubborn. Come out. I think we can work this all out," replied Gideon.

The ever-rational brother that he was, Gideon seemed to think that her aching heart was a problem easily solved if simply talked through using logic and then moving on. It would be cruel of her to point out that applying that to his own life wasn't working so well. Her brother could claim that he had pushed aside his hurt, losing Cordelia, but Emma knew the truth, and deep down so did he.

"Come in. It's not locked," said Emma.

"Come out."

Oh, for heaven's sake. Emma huffed and opened the door to admit him. His eyes widened when he saw her in their mother's dress. He stood there staring, then he smiled, his eyes shining with unshed tears.

"You...you look like Mama." His voice caught. "Just like her, Emma. You look beautiful."

Emma blushed. "Thank you." Her brother could have no idea how much his compliment meant to her. There were times that she missed her mother so much that she thought her heart was physically breaking. She could see on his face how much he grieved for their mother too.

On a whim, she twirled in a circle, and the soft layers of the dress spun around her.

Gideon shook his head. "I don't need a full dance, thanks."

Emma laughed. "I think that sometimes you boys forget I'm a girl at all."

He rubbed his forehead and shrugged. "We probably do. But you don't help yourself much with that." Gideon turned back and looked down the end of the hallway. "Anyway, I didn't come to see you play dress-up; there is someone here to see you."

Gideon averted his eyes and then strode back down the hallway. He didn't say who; he just expected her to follow. Apparently, his compliment didn't extend to courtesy. Rueful, but curious Emma trailed along behind him, wondering who'd arrived in the middle of a working day.

Still wearing their mother's gown, Emma walked past the rest of her open-mouthed brothers to the front door. She should have been having some quiet time in her bedroom, but Tilly had her hand on the doorknob and was staring at Emma in awe.

"You look BEE-Utiful, Auntie Emma!!!" Then she gave all three of her uncles a scowl. "Early says an open mouth is an invitation for flies!"

All three jaws snapped shut.

"Well?" asked Emma, as she looked around at her gathered family. "Who's here, and why are you all looking at me like I've grown a second head?"

Ben was the first to respond. "Sorry, Emma. We aren't trying to be rude. I think we are seeing for the first time that you're all grown up."

Emma blushed for the second time in as many minutes. She wasn't quite sure what to do with this version of her brothers. "Thank you, Ben." She nodded at Luke and Rhett. "Boys. Anyone care to show me where this visitor is hiding?"

Tilly was the quickest. Yanking the front door open as though revealing a prize, Tilly cried, "It's Mister Marshal Hayes!"

Emma hadn't dared to hope; the past twenty-four hours had taken their toll on her emotions. But there he was. Wes. Standing in the yard, freshly shaven, his wavy black hair smoothed down as best he could, and his hat in hand.

"Emma."

Wes took a step forward, then stopped. She watched as

his piercing blue eyes took in her appearance. His face read shock then appreciation. Emma gave silent thanks to her mother for the dress.

"You're back." Emma was trying to maintain her composure. Surely, there was no reason for him to return unless he had finally come to his senses. Could it be true?

There was not a sound from her brothers, and even Tilly was silent.

"I am," stated Wes. He began to fidget with the brim of his hat. He cleared his throat and spoke.

"The thing is. I guess I *do* want a headstrong, stubborn, drive-me-crazy kind of woman. One who is full of too many questions and determined to live life to the fullest."

Emma held up a hand. "Hold on there, Marshal. Are you sure that this is how you want to do this?"

Wes shook his head and kicked a toe into the dirt. "Honestly, Emma, I'm not sure of a darn thing anymore. Since the moment I saw you coming down Main Street in Autumn Springs, my whole life has been turned upside down, and I can't understand half of what I'm feeling."

His blue eyes full of sincerity, Wes continued. "But there is one thing I do know, Miss Emma Hart, and that's the thought of riding away from the Double H, and knowing that I would never see you again, made me feel about as sick as man could be. My stomach's been in knots since we parted." Wes took another breath. "See, I never thought I'd be bothering with all this. I've worked hard to avoid it. I figured that helping to bring a little justice to the world would be enough to fulfill me. That doing right, and dedicating myself to marshaling, would be enough. But it's not enough, not now that I've met you. If I hadn't, maybe I could have gone on thinking my soul was full, but I have met you, and I know now how wrong I was. Dead wrong, to think I could ever truly walk away from you."

Emma's heart warmed and the love she thought she would have to hide away forever cascaded though her, bringing a lightness and warmth that radiated from within. Wes had come back, and he'd come back for her. She didn't need to convince him to be here; he *wanted* to be with her.

"What are you trying to say?" Emma knew it, but her heart wanted to hear him say the words. She wanted him to say them out loud, the same way she wished to shout them out to the sky.

"What am I— What? Haven't you heard a single thing I said? How many more words do I need to say?"

Emma let out a soft laugh.

Wes shook his head. "Woman! If you didn't get all that, and I think you did, let me be perfectly clear what I'm about." He grinned sheepishly, realizing that she was having him on.

"I love you, Emma Hart, and I don't care who knows it. If I have to shout it to the world to make you understand, then that is exactly what I'll do."

"I don't think that will be necessary." Emma walked down the wide steps from the porch and stopped when she stood before him, looking up into his hopeful, smiling face. "I heard you just fine."

"I heard you too!" called out Tilly.

"We all did," added Ben, drily.

Emma watched as Wes tore his gaze from her and realized how big an audience his arrival had drawn.

Flushing, he looked back at her and chuckled. "I hadn't meant to make a spectacle."

"Well, you've certainly made yourself clear, and I appreciate that." Emma wiped at some imaginary dust on Wes's collar.

"So, you're not going to send me packing?" His voice was lower now, his words meant only for her. "I know I was a fool for leaving in the first place, for making things tougher than they needed to be. But I promise you that I will never leave you again. I love you, Emma."

Tears threatened as Emma met Wes's adoring gaze.

"I love you, too. From the first moment I saw you leaning against that post outside the lawyer's office. And when the door opened and I saw you standing out here, I knew that my heart could never stop loving, that I was a fool to think I could."

Wes grinned. "So, I didn't need to say all that? In front of everyone?"

"Oh, you most certainly did," laughed Emma.

Wes leaned in, and Emma was sure she was finally going to be kissed by the man she loved, when several throats cleared loudly behind her.

WES PULLED BACK, reminded by the army of Harts behind Emma what he had come here to do.

"I almost forgot. You weren't the only person I came to speak with here at the Double H today," said Wes.

Emma raised an eyebrow, in the way Wes had come to realize foreshadowed a flurry of questions.

"What does that mean? Who were you here to see? How long have you been here?" Emma indicated with a thumb over her shoulder. "Did they all know, and not tell me?"

"So many questions," chuckled Wes. "But this time you will have to have some patience while I ask one of my own."

Her eyes widened, and Wes was hard-pressed not to kiss her soundly right then and there. Instead, he motioned over to Gideon, Rhett, Ben, and Luke, standing together cross-armed on the porch. Only Tilly was grinning; the Hart brothers' faces remained neutral, waiting.

"You see, once I came to my senses—knowing that I couldn't live without you—I came straight to the Double H. I know how important family is to you, Emma, as it should be. I also know that, despite their teasing, your brothers love you and want you happy and safe. As do I."

Wes stopped to glance at the Harts, then, grinning, he looked back at Emma. "I'm my own man, Emma, and while I respect those men behind you, I'm not afraid of them."

Luke harrumphed then let out a yelp when Ben cuffed him upside the head with an open palm.

Wes ignored the theatrics behind Emma and continued. "So, I didn't come out here to ask their permission, but I did come out here, hoping to have their blessing. I got that, and now the final decision is yours alone to make."

Emma gasped as Wes sank down to one knee, placing his hat in the dust and dirt of the ranch yard.

"Oh, Emma." Wes gave a long sigh, his clear blue eyes meeting Emma's. "You have proven to be quite the distraction. I thought I was headed in one direction, but I was on the wrong path, and now I know where my place should be." He smiled. "That place is at your side and, God willing, having you at mine."

Wes gently took her hand in his. "Miss Emma Hart, will you please do me the greatest honor and become my wife?"

There was absolute silence around them, and even the birds fell quiet, as though they too awaited her answer.

"Yes," whispered Emma.

"Yes?"

"Yes, yes, yes! I would be happy to be your wife," replied Emma joyfully. She smoothed down the layers of her mother's blue dress as Wes rose to his feet. He dusted his hat off as he put it back on and pulled her into his arms.

"I don't think I've ever seen you look more beautiful." His voice came out a low rumble, meant for her ears alone.

"I think it might be the first time you've actually seen me clean and dressed like a lady should be," replied Emma.

"There is no denying your beauty in this dress, Emma, but my lady should dress any way she chooses, and I will always consider myself the luckiest of men."

"That's a really good answer, Wes."

"I'm learning." And he was. Emma was to be his partner, not his property, and he wanted her to know that he understood that fact.

She returned his embrace, and placed her cheek against his chest. It was then, with Emma in his arms, that Wes felt a peace that he hadn't even known he was searching for. She fit just right, like the piece that had been missing. Like it was always meant to be.

"I love you, Emma." Wes whispered the words into the smooth, dark hair of the head that rested against him.

"I love you too."

Before she could say any more, Wes removed his hat and, turning it sideways to shield their faces from her brothers, he caught Emma's chin and turned her head to face him. Seeing his joy and love reflected in her gaze, he tenderly touched his lips to hers. Surprised, she was hesitant at first, but then her body pressed against his as their kiss deepened. Her passion warmed him to his very core.

Pulling back, Wes placed his hat back on his head and smiled. This time there were no clearing throats, only the cheers of the Hart family.

EPILOGUE

L aughter rang out, filling the great room of the ranch house.

Emma didn't think she could be any happier. Before she had said 'I do' in front of the preacher, there was an ever-so-brief moment of sadness that she was giving up her Hart surname, but one look at the adoring face of her new husband, and she knew that being Mrs. Weston Hayes had been her destiny. This day could only have been made better by the arrival of her brother Micah. The Harts had been expecting him days ago, but there had been unforeseen delays, and he still wasn't home. It would have been absolutely perfect to have all five of her brothers back together on this day, but selfishly, Emma wasn't putting off becoming Wes's bride a day longer.

The boys were ribbing each other, and it was only when Luke made a jest about adding cowbells to the springs of the newlyweds' nuptial bed, and Nora's face flamed, that Emma disrupted the festivities. Her brothers had been on their best behavior during the simple homespun ceremony, but that had been hours ago, and decorum had left with the minister.

"Enough of that, now. You are still in mixed company, *Gentlemen*." Her emphasis on that designation was more of a question.

"Forgive us, Emma," said Ben. "I think we were all wondering if you were going to become an old maid."

"That's cheeky talk, coming from my *elder*, and as yet, unattached brother," scoffed Emma.

"Older, not elderly; there's a difference!" defended Ben, his laughter as big as he was.

"Careful there, Ben," Wes quipped. "It happens quick. You think your days of running solo will never end, but then you meet that one gal, and just like that, you're hitched."

Luke held up his hands, as if to hold back such a fate. "Speak for yourself, Deputy. You're the only one crazy enough to say yes. A lawman issuing his own life sentence. Who knew?"

Wes chuckled at his new brother-in-law, unfazed by the jab. He'd taken quickly to the life of a large family and was giving her brothers back as good as he got.

"Mark my words. Matrimonial bliss is coming for you too," Wes warned.

"Guess I'd better lie low then," said Luke, grinning, a murmur of agreement coming from the other men.

"Ha! Good luck to you all. When love comes calling, you'll have no choice but to answer," he laughed.

Wes's declaration was met with a chorus of laughter and dismissal, but Emma knew just how wrong her brothers were. Family was everything to the Harts, and when each brother found the right woman, she knew they would let nothing stop them from taking that plunge. The only question was, which of them would be the first to fall?

As the men joked, Emma turned to admire her best friend. Nora's blonde hair was tucked up in a simple bun with soft tendrils falling to either side, framing her pretty face. Her calico dress of light grey flowers with a snug bodice was topped with an intricately crocheted collar that could only have been the handiwork of Nora's talented mother.

Nora would never admit it, but Emma knew that her friend had also hoped Micah would be home for the wedding and had taken extra care with her appearance, not only for the celebratory occasion, but in the off-chance he was still able to make it. They were all disappointed when he hadn't. Emma was excited for the reunion between the two. With Micah back for good, Emma expected that it wouldn't be long before she was helping Nora prepare for her own happy day.

"Thank you so much for everything. You're the best of friends. You always have been."

"Of course," Nora said, smiling. "I think it's been almost as much fun for me as it has for you. I had a feeling this is where you'd end up from that first day you came tearing over to tell me about Weston."

Emma still blushed at the memory of meeting Wes in the Garvin Mercantile.

"Do you remember when we used to throw apple peels over our shoulders? That however they landed would magically show the initials of our husbands to be?" asked Emma.

Nora giggled. "I do. Although I don't think I ever saw anything that looked like a 'W' for you."

Grinning, Emma replied, "I know! I was terrible at peeling and had nothing but short, straight strips. I thought it meant 'I' and that unless I married myself, I would never get to say my vows."

"Not true!" Nora countered. "I recall you crying all after-noon because you thought you were destined to marry Ignatius Barnes. I still remember how relieved you were when his family moved back east the following year."

"Ugh, Iggy Barnes, that boy could hardly keep his finger out of his nose! I certainly wasn't going to let him put a ring on mine."

"Poor Iggy," laughed Nora.

Emma shook her head at her friend. "Sometimes I wish your memory wasn't so keen. I was finally starting to forget about that."

"Someone has to keep you honest," said Nora, impishly. Then, she glanced over to Emma's husband. "Although I guess I'm passing that honor to Weston now."

Nora leaned over and nudged her shoulder against Emma's. "I'm so happy for you. He's a good man, and the right fit for you. Aren't you glad you never settled?"

"Thank you, Nora. He really is, and I really am," agreed Emma. "I am over the moon. There were moments today when I was so happy, I thought I might faint."

Nora giggled again. "It's probably that corset. We tied you in there so tightly, I'm impressed you didn't swoon halfway through the preacher's final speech."

"I almost did, with the heat of the day. And I'm dying to lift my arms beyond my elbows."

"But you look absolutely enchanting. It must be worth it."

Emma pretended to take an impossible deep breath and softly gasped a reply. "It is." Both women laughed.

Emma definitely wasn't complaining.

Between the needlework talents of Teresa and Nora, and Emma's enthusiastic moral support, they had created a wedding gown for her that looked like it could have walked right off the pages of a ladies fashion journal.

Unlike her mother's, it was a soft cream color that was apparently becoming all the rage. The fabric was made in a novelty weave, both plain and satin. Running down the sides of the skirt were silk panels that showcased Teresa's delicate embroidery, tiny flowers cascading downward.

Emma conceded to wearing the corset, but decried the expected bustle, stating it was an unnecessary addition to her already-ample natural endowments. The lace frill that ran down the bodice and edged both collar and sleeves was exquisite, and it ensured that Emma felt like the most radiant of brides.

After a full afternoon, and with night arriving, the beautiful gown was becoming more and more uncomfortable, but Emma had promised herself, as well as Nora and Teresa, that she wouldn't complain. For at least this one day, Wes would have a shining example on his arm of what a lady should look like.

Her brothers were now debating about whether to join the other men out at the bunkhouse. Lee Manning had buried a bottle of bourbon a month prior when the date of Emma's nuptials had been announced. According to his family's southern tradition, the buried bottle would ensure a wedding day free of rain. The superstition worked as there wasn't a drop to be found, and now the men had dug it up and were enjoying the one evening when Gideon waived the 'dry' bunkhouse rule.

Before the men left, Wes stood up and announced that he had something he wanted to share. This surprised Emma, as he hadn't said a word to her about any news. The only happening she could think of was his acceptance of the deputy sheriff's position in Autumn Springs. But everyone in this room already knew of that.

Reminding herself to practice patience, Emma waited for Wes to speak.

He stood up and, walking over to the chair where he'd taken off his wedding coat, he pulled an envelope from the inner pocket. Emma was as much in the dark as everyone else in the room, but she could tell that whatever Wes was up to, he was quite pleased with himself.

He waved the envelope around with a flourish to the curious crowd.

"Now, I suppose you're wondering what I have here in my hand? I can guarantee that my beautiful wife is." The room filled with laughter and Wes glanced in her direction. "I can't tell you how happy that word makes me."

"Me too," replied Emma, her cheeks rosy with Wes's compliment.

"All of us here know how much our dear Emma longs for adventure ... of the safe variety now." Wes sent her a wink. "And I was hoping that the ever-absent Micah would have arrived by now, so that we might have met before I did this, but a wedding gift really should be given on one's wedding day. And I fear that I would not have been able to hide this from her much longer."

There was more laughter in the room, to which Emma replied, "Are you practicing your speeches for when you run for sheriff? Get on with it!"

Shouts of agreement went around the room, until Gideon shot everyone a glare and warned his siblings not to wake up his daughter.

"Fair enough," laughed Wes, and he placed the envelope in Emma's hands and waited for her to open it.

Emma broke the seal and, reaching in, she then pulled out two train tickets. She was confused. "What are these for?"

"Those, my love, are just the beginning of our adventure together." Wes smiled down at her. "I'm taking you on a grand tour, Mrs. Hayes. You're going to see big cities, go to a real theater, eat strange foods, and see the ocean. And hear me now. I promise, that even if it mortifies the locals, I will stand guard as you strip off your stockings and dip your bare toes in the ocean."

Nora clasped the bouquet she had caught earlier to her chest in delight, and one of Emma's brothers gave out a low whistle.

Emma was speechless, shocked by what she heard. She was having a hard time comprehending the enormity of this gift. It wasn't only that she would have a chance to experience the things she only thought to dream of; it was that Wes had listened to her. He'd heard her and remembered what she'd said.

This man who had once been so sure that he wouldn't share his life with another had somehow transformed himself into the perfect husband, and he had only been married for one day.

Emma placed the tickets on a table behind her and with subtle assistance from Nora, stood up from her chair, her eyes wet with unshed tears.

Wes took her hands in his. "You like it? You're happy?"

Eyes glistening, Emma pushed through the thickness in her throat to speak. "Oh, Wes, how could I not? You're ... it's perfect."

He nodded. "Good. With everything that happened, I didn't want you to ever worry that I might want to change you." He placed his thumb beneath her chin so that her brown eyes met his gaze of blue. "I love your sense of wonder and adventure, and you don't have to ever lose that enthusiasm, for me or for anyone."

Emma thought her heart might burst. Wes's thoughtfulness moved her in a way she couldn't define. There were no words to describe the moment you knew that you were unconditionally loved. That who you are is okay, that who she was, was enough.

The intensity of her emotions threatened to spill over, when a thought struck her.

"But how? How can you—did you—"

"Afford my grand plan?" chuckled Wes.

Cheeks red with embarrassment, Emma nodded. She didn't think that Wes's previous life as a deputy US marshal could warrant such luxury.

"I've filled some lucrative contracts and for most of those lonely years I spent my nights under the stars." Wes smiled. "And from that smile on your face, each one of them has been worth it, if only for this moment, right here."

Emma, still amazed by it all, only wanted to feel her husband's warm embrace. She leaned into him, Wes wrapping his strong arms around her, when the front door was thrown open, and a booming voice shouted, "I object!"

Micah, grinning, charged through the door, his boots clacking on the flagstone floor as he strode in, greeting his brothers in passing and accepting an enthusiastic bearhug from his twin.

Emma couldn't believe he was here! Micah had finally made it home.

She turned to see Nora, her face a mixture of joy and uncertainty. Emma moved to grab her hand, but her friend was nervously moving to the back of the room.

"Am I too late?" asked Micah. "I'm not sure I like the look of him."

Wes laughed and extended his hand, which Micah took and shook unreservedly. "Welcome home, Micah."

"I guess I should say the same to you; it's good to finally meet you. I don't know whether to call you Marshal or Deputy. My information isn't always current."

"Wes works fine," replied her husband.

Emma was so happy to have all of her brothers home, together. The day could not have ended on a better note.

"When did you get in?" asked Luke. "Why didn't you send word?"

"We only arrived a few hours ago," replied Micah.

"We?" asked Emma. What did he mean by *we*? His face was shining, and Emma started to get a sinking feeling in her stomach.

Micah grinned, his twinkling eyes watching Luke's confused ones. "I told you I had exciting news," said Micah.

Oh no. No, no, no. Emma prayed that Micah would stop talking. That he wouldn't say what she feared was coming.

He didn't stop.

"I'm getting married!" he exclaimed.

Emma's heart dropped. She didn't need to see Nora's face to know what was there. This was the last thing that Emma had expected. She couldn't even begin to imagine what Nora was feeling with Micah's stunning announcement.

There was only a low murmur of congratulations, and Micah's brow furrowed. "I thought I would get a better reception that this. Now I'm glad Isabelle was too tired from her travel to meet you all tonight. Aren't you all happy for me?"

"I'm sure we are all very happy for you." Nora stepped out from where she had been standing behind Ben. "The ...

news was just ... unexpected. Congratulations, Micah. I wish you every happiness."

Nora's face was pale, but she held herself straight. Emma was amazed by the strength her friend was showing. She was magnificent in the face of such devastating news.

Micah's face was equally colorless.

"Nora! I didn't ... I didn't see you there."

"Obviously," growled Luke, as he scowled at his twin and walked over to stand beside Nora.

The air in the room had gone still. Thankfully, Gideon was able to find his tongue. "Nora's right. Congratulations, Micah. It's good to have you home."

Micah nodded, but his eyes were still on Nora.

Emma wanted to whack her brother upside the head for his ignorance but, remembering her promise to remain a lady, she held back.

"Luke," said Emma, regaining her poise. "Why don't you take Nora back home. I'm sure her poor mother is expecting her."

"Gladly," grunted Luke.

Nora gave Emma a grateful look. "Thank you. Yes. I really should be getting back, and this way your family can be together."

Luke quickly spoke up. "You are—"

Nora interrupted Luke by placing her hand on his arm. "We should go, Luke."

Nora passed the bridal bouquet she had caught to Luke as she hugged Emma goodbye.

The women didn't speak; this wasn't the time or place.

As Luke and Nora left the room, they had to pass Micah. Nora nodded at him, but Luke wasn't so civil.

He shoved the delicate bundle of flowers against Micah's chest. "Here, why don't you give these to your fiancée."

And, leaving Micah holding the bouquet, he stomped out the door.

WILL Nora and Micah find their way back to each other? Grab your copy of **MICAH'S HONOR** and find out!

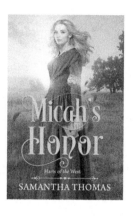

Made in the USA
Monee, IL
07 June 2023

35211544R00115